IMMERSION

IMMERSION

MARY MACKEY

iUniverse, Inc.
Bloomington

IMMERSION

IMMERSION

PREFACE

First published in 1972 by Alta Gerry's legendary Shameless Hussy Press, Mary Mackey's *Immersion* was a ground-breaking novel, decades ahead of its time. In an era when "ecology" was still a word so unfamiliar that some were still spelling it "ekology", Mackey chose to make the ecology of the tropical rain forest of Costa Rica one of her primary themes, depicting the beauty and fragility of a complex natural ecosystem endangered by human incursions. Her other great theme is Kirsten's rebellion against traditional female roles. Kirsten's liberation is intellectual, spiritual, personal, and sexual. In many ways, she seems more a woman of the early 21st Century than a woman of her own time, and in creating her Mackey gives us a vision of the early stages of Second Wave feminism.

Immersion was the first feminist novel published by a Second Wave feminist press, and is thus quite possibly the first eco-feminist novel ever published. After *Immersion*, Mackey wrote twelve subsequent novels and six collections of poetry, many of which contain that same remarkable combination of mystical lyricism and intense scientific observation which at times seems almost prophetic.

Eduardo is drowning.

Rocking from side to side, he moves like a swimmer—head up, eyes open, fingers pressed tightly together. A neurotoxin is paralyzing his central nervous system, depressing respiration, sending his body into a series of involuntary convulsions.

The boy opens his mouth; his throat constricts spasmodically, forcing his head down against his chest. Choking on air, he coughs up an invisible stream of bubbles—broken, discontinuous, incomplete.

Arching his back, Eduardo lifts himself away from the ground, pushing up towards an imaginary surface. Rising slowly, carried by an unseen current, he seems to move towards a kind of temporary equilibrium.

(Closing my eyes, I stop the motion, reducing it to a static image. The memory emerges as a perfect reflection, clear, motionless, undistorted. Eduardo appears in front of me, his head turned slightly to one side. In the large muscles, just below his neck, I can see two symmetrical punctures. The marks are clean, deep, uninflamed; the venom has been injected almost without a trace.)

Eduardo throws his arms out to either side and rolls over on his back.

(Closing my eyes, I stop the motion, reverse the sequence.)

♦ ♦ ♦

Inside the cabin, behind the green nylon screen, Mark bends over the table. In his right hand, pinched between the tips of his thumb and first two fingers, he is holding a single-edge razor blade. This blade is projected onto the surface of the table as a short, blunt line, a small black band that intersects the cracks between the boards at an acute angle. Seen from above, it appears as a condensation and distortion of the original object; height has been transformed into width, into a slight thickening and blurring of the original object.

Mark tilts the blade, bending his fingers at the second joint, pulling the back corner (rusty along the lower edge, nicked at the extreme point of the tip) in towards the palm of his hand, moving it towards the mound of flesh just below his thumb. Bending closer to the bird, he flexes his wrist in a perfect semi-circle, bringing the edge of the blade in contact with the body, making a narrow, precise incision along the abdomen. Turning slightly, he runs the tip between fat and feathers, methodically severing the bands of connective tissue.

Mark pushes back the skin rapidly, automatically, as if he were peeling a small fruit. The bare flesh is exposed, shining, slick, covered with a thin white membrane, suspended behind it like a fetus floating in amniotic fluid.

Without looking up from the bird, Mark reaches into a small, unglazed bowl, removes a handful of coarse yellow powder, and throws it into the open incision.

(The bowl is projected onto the table as a two-dimensional crescent; the actual bottom (composed of glossy brown clay, rising above the shadow) intersects the outer edge of the reflected circle, forming a concentric arc, interrupting the continuity of the rim, as

8

if a portion of the light had been solidified, colored, rotated through an extra dimension.)

As they fall between the layers of fat and skin, the grains of cornmeal expand, become denser, cling together, absorb and retain fat, blood, and fluids from the partially skinned bird. Mark reaches out again. Picking up a short wooden rod, he wraps it in several layers of dry surgical cotton, pushes the empty skin over the stuffing, and pulls the irregular edges of the incision together. Without pausing or altering the position of his body, he begins to sew up the abdomen with a piece of black cotton thread, smoothing down the blue and green feathers, pulling them over the stitches with the first two fingers of his left hand.

As he lifts his head, Mark's face is suddenly illuminated; every detail (exposed and expanded) is revealed with microscopic clarity. A few fragments of gray down float across it, moving out of his field of vision, sucked up out of the circle of light by invisible currents.

(The fragments turn, casting minute, indistinct shadows across Mark's cheeks and forehead, along his chin and the bridge of his nose; they revolve slowly, as if suspended in a heavy, transparent liquid—small, elaborately carved particles, bits of shell and coral floating to the surface, hollow, serrated, branched, pointed at the tips.)

Mark bends over the table. He does not appear to notice the drifting specks of down.

♦ ♦ ♦

The mail plane (two hours out of Puerto Viejo) is flying inland, following the Rio Culebra away from the coast. As the sun moves toward the center of the sky, the river becomes an intense blinding strip of light, a band of molten tin interrupted by indistinct clusters, by broken black lines that seem to drift randomly across the surface. On either side, the rain forest stretches out to the horizon, covering the ground with a sheet of green enamel (flat, motionless, congealed), a dense, impervious veneer of overlapping leaves. From time to time (disturbed by the noise of the motor) a large bird rises suddenly out of the canopy, moving up towards the plane in a rapid, steady spiral. Then (abandoning the convection currents, passing through the cross-shaped shadow of the vanishing Cessna) it folds its wings and plummets back beneath the surface.

Mark leans towards the window, turning away from Kirsten, moving his body slowly, methodically. Holding onto the window frame with one hand, he braces his legs stiffly against the struts. Below the tip of the right wing, the clearing appears as a chip in the vegetation, a roughly peltate depression attached to the river by half a mile of dirt road. Farther upstream, the land has been logged over. Piles of timber lie rotting on the ground.

(The Lumber Company left because of the river. Flooding suddenly, without any apparent cause, it cut new paths through the forest, washing away docks and piers, creating (overnight) vast, stagnant lakes; splicing together endless channels where the logs (trapped under overhanging trees, moving in immense overlapping epicycles, perpetually repeating the same configurations) decayed in the water, or (propelled by invisible currents into endless diverticula) were lost before they could reach the ocean.)

10

As the plane dips lower, approaching the clearing, the river becomes an incandescent band; the forest is broken into irregular segments, into two lozenges soldered by a bright metallic seam. The horizon (detached by the rapid descent) rises up above both wings. Mark leans back and tightens his seatbelt. The wheels hit the ground roughly, throwing him forward against the pilot's seat. As he straightens up, he can see a segment of the forest through the windshield. The trees appear to move, distorted by the invisible blades of the propeller, stroboscopic, unstable.

As the motor stops, the scene slowly congeals, crystallizing at the edges. The trees (immobile, fixed rigidly in a semi-circle) look like giant stalagmites. Mark reaches down and unhooks his belt. As he straightens up again, a boy and a girl appear at the edge of the clearing.

♦ ♦ ♦

The cabin is at the far edge of the clearing, peripheral to the forest which extends (as a single, green, unbroken wave) beyond memory, beyond action, beyond imagination.

Inside, behind the nylon screen, two people are sitting at a small wooden table, eating black beans, rice, and goat cheese. The cheese has been sliced and fried, each piece coated with a colorless film of oil that drips into shallow pools at the corners. Near the opposite edge of the table, separated as far as possible from the plates and bottles, there is a half-used box of matches, a spool of black cotton thread, two dead birds, and an unlighted kerosene lamp.

The man and woman eat silently, eat without looking up from their plates, manipulating the food with almost mechanical efficiency. Both are wearing faded work shirts, khaki pants, high leather boots, and dirty wool socks. The socks have been rolled down over the tops of the boots, concealing the upper portion of the lacing.

Despite the fact that they are eating dinner, both the man and woman are carrying a canteen and a machete slung from their belts. The man (hunched over the table) is somewhere in his late thirties, short, partially bald. His chest and shoulders are solid, thick; his nose blunt; his lips wide, flat, folded loosely over his front teeth. As he reaches out to pick up the box of matches, his arms (distorted by the falling light) appear to stretch, to move away from his body like the crooked falces of an immense spider.

The woman (sitting with her back to the door) is several years younger. In the semi-darkness, her face appears as a small gray oval; a single, featureless surface. Her hair is tied back from her forehead with a blue and white bandanna folded into a triangle.

Putting up his pocket knife with a slight, mechanical click, Mark reaches across the table, removes the shade from the lamp, and turns up the cotton wick. Without lifting her head, Kirsten pushes her plate to one side and begins to pick splinters out of the table with the prongs of her fork, bending the right one slightly until it curves counterclockwise, touching the outer edge of the middle tine.

Mark's hands appear to be two different sizes. As he leans forward to light the lamp, one seems partially flattened, as though it had been pressed between heavy weights. The other—blunter, foreshortened from the tips of the fingers to the wrist—looks more compact, denser, moves more rapidly in a series of discontinuous, tentative arcs.

Mark picks up the match box and pushes out the tray with a quick flick of his index finger. In the dim light, the box is reduced to a rectangle, a one-dimensional lozenge bordered by a blurred white hand.

◆ ◆ ◆

Night. I pick my way blindly across the clearing, anticipating (mechanically, by memory) each bend in the path. I walk slowly, pushing aside the tall, wet grass, forcing my way through the dense underbrush along the river. The leaves (sliding over my fingers and wrists, brushing against the palms of my hands) feel like sheets of stiff plastic—broad, flat, resilient. They blend together invisibly in the darkness, forming a series of overlapping textures, a tactile continuum of surfaces and consistencies. I move through them deliberately, surrounded by an oval of absolute silence.

The oval moves with me. On all sides, the frogs and insects stop, frozen, suddenly mute, concealed in the shadows. Their calls are abruptly interrupted, suspended temporarily. Behind me, I hear them begin again. The sounds are resumed at a reduced volume. They seem to be coming from a great distance, passing through an invisible barrier, muted, and softened. As territorial boundaries are reestablished, antiphonic patterns appear. Twigs snap; something slides into the river with a slight splash.

Entering the forest, I sense a change in the temperature and density of the air. The shadows seem to grow thicker, to curve around me, conforming to my body like sheets of black glass. My boots scrape against a root. The sound is not conducted, not propagated or transmitted; it is absorbed immediately, extinguished at its source.

At the edge of the river, I stop, reach up, and turn on my headlamp. The light spreads out in a wide, pale circle, barely penetrating the darkness, creating a vague, deceptive landscape of multiple shadows. Small plants are enlarged, projected all out of proportion. Only parts of things are visible—a shred of Heliconia (one disembodied bract suspended from an invisible

14

axis), a section of balsa trunk (white, smooth, rounded at either end, hanging in space like a strip of paper), half a flower (bloated, asymmetrical, twisting back and forth in the flickering light like a deformed moth).

As I move along the bank, the pieces change, modified by my headlamp, transformed by the shifting angle of the beam. Streaming in front of me in a continuous band, the plants blend together, forming a ribbon of indistinct after-images, fluid, formless splotches of color. Abstract, unrecognizable forms float past on both sides, merge and separate, without continuity or depth. The forest is broken, disconnected, cut into meaningless fragments by the moving light.

(Walking slowly upstream, Kirsten forces her way through the dense brush, pushing aside the overhanging leaves.)

Plants and animals pass into one another, a perpetual metempsychosis of protective coloration. Forms, colors, and patterns converge generating an organic colloid; foreground and background blend by mutual accommodation.

A stick is floating down the river, drifting towards the pool below the bridge. As it passes the edge of the gravel triangle (just below the mouth of the creek), it suddenly turns, slides up the bank, and coils itself around a warm rock. As it dries in the sun, the bark begins to turn to scales.

At the top of the guayabo tree, a flock of green fruits pecks at crawling twigs and flying seeds. Black and yellow vines twist over the branches, move down the trunk and out along the prop roots.

For an instant, the camouflage is lifted. Bees are exposed as flies, their long stingers transformed into harmless ovipositors. An ant becomes a spider disguised to hunt ants. As it moves from one log to another, an owl is changed into a Caligo butterfly with eyespots on each wing. The snout of a huge weasel (seen from above, clearly, without an apparent discontinuity) is only the body of a muff bat covered with a hood of gray and white fur.

The delicate petals and stamens of plants fold up their wings, fly out of the flowers, become plume-moths, become the pro-thoraxes of immense mantids. To lure them back, the plants, in turn, imitate the sexual organs of female moths, the movements of small insects, the smell of rotting meat.

Below this vast system of overlapping forms, the river flows towards the bridge, a strip of clear water that imitates (by reflection) the forest canopy, that mimics (as a mirror mimics) the overhanging trees, the broad,

parallel-veined leaves, the empty, green, glossed arc of
the sky.

✦ ✦ ✦

(A kind of constant clearness suspends my mind just above the surface of its actions, a sheet of green glass, translucent, curving out infinitely in all directions. Everything I remember seems to have taken place below this barrier, submerged, under water.)

Salamander Cave, southern Indiana.

A small tunnel stretches off to the right of the central chamber. The entrance is partially blocked by breakdown, concealed under a heap of limestone that has fallen from the roof. A cold draft comes out of the mouth of the hole. As one of the men bends down to pick up a piece of quartz, his hair is blown back from his face.

Kirsten unzips her windbreaker and hangs it on a stalagmite. Then she unstraps her hardhat and puts it on top of the jacket. Placing a plastic bottle (full of carbide) and a canteen at the bottom of the pile, she turns and begins to walk toward the tunnel. One of the men says something in a low voice. Without looking up, Kirsten falls to her knees and crawls part way into the opening. Pressing her arms to her sides (elbows in, hands clenched) she pulls herself forward, disappearing completely.

One of the men sits down and takes off his headlamp. Blowing out the flame, he unscrews the top and empties out a pile of gray ash. The ash (damp, coherent) sticks to the side of the rock, staining it slightly. The man refills his lamp with carbide and checks the water supply. Replacing the top (screwing it down clockwise, forcing it over the rusty threads) he lifts the lamp to his face, holding the reflector just below his nose.

There is a faint odor of acetylene. The man probes the hole with a piece of wire. The odor grows stronger. Holding the lamp at arm's length, he strikes

18

the flint. A bright white flame shoots out of the center
of the lamp. Multiplied by the reflector, it projects
enormous shadows on the opposite wall of the central
chamber.

◆ ◆ ◆

I am aware of small perturbations, changes so slight that they seem to have been imagined.

(My husband is sitting at a table preparing some study skins. As he leans forward to adjust the lamp, I am conscious of the sudden contraction of his pupils, the shallow rhythm of his breathing, the temperature and texture of his skin. The light seems to penetrate his face, to cut through the flesh, revealing (just below the surface) a framework of transparent bones.)

The transition is so subtle that I perceive it only indirectly, parallactically, as if the entire system had changed its location without altering its composition, had been shifted several degrees while preserving (without perturbation) its internal structure. I sense (without being able to determine the source of this sensation) that something is happening—or perhaps more accurately, that something has happened. Suddenly, without warning, I am caught up in the development of a process, involved in a change of undetermined magnitude and direction.

(I feel myself moving away from Mark. There is a pause, a separation. I detach myself completely. reaching out with his right hand, he turns the knob on the base of the lamp clockwise. The flame flares up against the side of the shade. I watch him dispassionately, from a great distance, noting the composition and distribution of his features—the slope of his forehead, the curve of his jaw, the dark triangular patches of skin below each cheekbone. Effortlessly, as if by instinct, I observed the placement of the major muscles, the tense, rapid contraction of his lips and nostrils. Mark leans back in his chair, tilting the front legs off the floor. His face (obscured by the shadows) loses its contours. Blurring into the background, it appears as a smooth oval, a flat, blank surface.)

Without any apparent cause, I experience a shift in perspective, a radical change in the angle and focus of my perceptions. Visually, this shift is recognized as an intensification of outline. Objects seem brighter, more distinct; they appear as holographic projections, present in all dimensions. The space they occupy looks dense, slightly opaque, as if it were preserving (at a constant temperature and pressure) a kind of hydrostatic equilibrium. I feel myself floating through it, drifting away from Mark, condensed, self-contained, autonomous.

(Mark turns towards me. I recognize him just as one might recognize a plant or an animal, without observing individual deviations from type, noting only the general characteristics of his face, the arbitrary parameters of his body. On all sides of his head, radiating out from the periphery like a corona, I see (precisely, completely, with perfect clarity) the rest of the room. Except for certain differences in extension and position, the laws of perspective seem suspended. Everything exists in the same plane, projected onto a single surface. I have the impression that I am looking through a wide-angle telescope, through a lens that magnifies the intensity of my vision without narrowing its scope.)

I no longer occupy the same position relative to my surroundings; I perceive them differently, through a different medium.

(The interior of the cabin solidifies, crystallizing around the nets and birds, around the cots and along the edges of the table. Mark is caught at the center, trapped like an insect in a lump of amber. His arms are bent slightly, palms flat, fingers pressed together, frozen accidentally in a gesture of supplication.)

♦ ♦ ♦

Dulce-Maria is standing on the porch, looking through the nylon screen. In her right hand, she is holding a dented tin basin (white enamel, narrow blue stripes around the rim, cracked and chipped along bottom and sides). In the basin there are several large, parallel-veined leaves. In the other hand, the girl clutches the neck of a sisal bag, winding her first three fingers through the upper end of the webbing. The bag swings back and forth, scraping the edge of her left leg just below the knee, leaving a band of small red scratches. As the scratches begin to disappear, they form a net of broken white lines.

Beneath the leaves, concealed in the bottom of the basin, there are several small brown eggs, a dozen corn tortillas, and a wedge of white cheese. One of the eggs is cracked at the tip, exposing a thin, transparent membrane just below the shell. The membrane is stretched tightly across the crack like a water-tight seal.

Dulce-Maria moves closer to the door. She bends down slowly, keeping her back rigid, and gently lowers the basin to the floor. Then she unwinds her fingers from the neck of the bag and pushes it into a corner. Standing again, she reaches up, grabs a few loose strands of hair, and begins to wind them around her index finger, rolling them into a compact spiral.

As Dulce-Maria rotates her finger, two sets of shadows are projected onto the surface of the porch. To the left and right, her motions are repeated on the bare planks, extended into finer secondary shadows which duplicate the reflections of the original action. At the edge there is a kind of infinite regress of two-dimensional reproductions. Taken altogether, the shadows form a complex, overlapping system of moving silhouettes. Distance is reduced to foreshortening; depth appears as length; detail is entirely eliminated.

Without planning or changing the angle of her motion, Dulce-Maria opens her mouth slightly, reaches forward, and draws the curl between her lips, wetting it with the edge of her tongue. This motion—confined to the center of the silhouette—cannot be reproduced in the shadows.

Dulce-Maria continues to look through the door. Her eyes seem to be focused beyond the screen.

◆ ◆ ◆

As I become more visually aware of Mark, as I seem him (physically, concretely) with greater clarity, his emotional presence is reduced. I find that, somehow, I no longer experience him as an influence, perceive him as a focus of reaction, a point of constant perturbation.

(He leans forward to adjust the lamp, supporting himself against the edge of the table. As he moves towards me, every detail of his face (floating, disembodied, incorporeal) is exposed, expanded, magnified. It is as if, passing through a lens of intense white light, the boundaries—cheeks, chin, forehead— had been enlarged, stretched across a photo-sensitive surface, fixed beyond their normal limits. As he turns up the wick, the contrast is intensified. Black patches appear on either jaw, below the lip, at the rim of each nostril. For an instant, I have the impression that I am looking at a skull, a globe of bone with empty eye sockets. The face itself (moving back into the shadows) no longer seems to belong to anyone I have known.)

As it floats upwards, the body appears to swell, to become brighter, more distinct. The eyes appear; lashes are formed along the rims of the lids; mouth, nose, and chin emerge slowly, condensing as the face approaches the surface of the pool.

Equilibrium.

Lying flat on her back, Dulce-Maria floats with her arms flung out to either side—neck arched, toes pointed, ankles locked together. Her body (thin, hard, hairless—the strong, flat body of an eight-year-old girl) is bent backwards like a strip of rigid plastic, lifted off the surface of the water by its own tension.

The curve relaxes. Dulce-Maria straightens her spine, lifts one shoulder, and (turning abruptly, throwing her head forward like a lizard) dives below the surface.

The pool appears to be empty.

Without looking up, Eduardo continues to sharpen his machete, scraping against the stone rhythmically with a peculiar rocking motion. As he works, he smokes a few shreds of tobacco rolled up in a piece of brown wrapping paper. The cigarette (short, pinched at both ends) is glued together along one side with some sort of colorless vegetable gum. It burns unevenly, leaving a long pointed scrap of charred paper at the tip. From time to time, the boy inhales slowly, pinching the paper between his lips, blowing the smoke out through his nostrils. The action seems to be a kind of reflex, involuntary, unconscious.

Eduardo does not seem to notice that his sister has disappeared below the surface of the pool. Holding the machete by the handle (palm curved sideways, perpendicular to the broad edge of the blade) he places the fingers of his opposite hand lightly on the tip. Dragging the blade across the rough face of the rock with a circular motion, Eduardo presses the edge down, pushes it away, draws it back to its original position. He works steadily, with an almost mechanical precision, oblivious to everything but the knife, hypnotized by the moving blade. The rest of his body (naked, rigid, bent forward over the rock) is motionless, as though he were contemplating his actions from a distance, watching his fingers, palms, and wrists through a sheet of resin.

Something begins to move below the surface of the water, to recondense section by section.

Pushing the blade back and forth across the rock, Eduardo never alters the rhythm of the strokes, never changes their angle or intensity. He appears to be involved in some sort of religious ritual, powerless to extract himself, bound (by some invisible force) to the perfect repetition of the original pattern.

The tension is broken. Dulce-Maria appears at the far edge of the pool.

Without indication that he is aware of her presence, Eduardo continues to sharpen his machete. As he bends forward, frozen over the moving blade, a streak of sweat runs down his cheek. Thousands of tiny drops of water (caught in the fine hairs that cover his neck, back, and chest) shine in the sunlight, coating his body with a layer of wet varnish.

Behind him, unobserved, Dulce-Maria is floating on the surface of the pool, her arms flung out to either side.

♦ ♦ ♦

Lying beside me (rigid, immobile, both legs thrust out stiffly over the edge of the cot) Mark moves away at a constant velocity, blending into the background, receding into an indefinite volume. Despite his physical presence, despite the constant, balanced rhythm of his breathing, he is reduced to an object, to a solid curve described above the surface of the bed, an arc subtended by a chord.

The lamp goes out completely.

There is a sudden transition from visual to aural, an abrupt attenuation of color and form. Mark's face appears clearly for a moment, floating in front of me like an incipient hallucination, a negative after-image, suspended, shrinking, isolated. Then it breaks into fragments. Each detail becomes an independent point of focus, detached from the whole, a random particle moving without a center, without connection, without recurrence.

I feel myself drifting away from him, floating out into the darkness. I am weightless and invisible. I have escaped (spontaneously, without contrivance or design) from his influence, from the centripetal force of his body.

Mark no longer exists.

(He turns in his sleep, pushing up against me, throwing his left arm across my chest. Reduced to a few simple lines, to the serial intrusions of a strictly tactile trajectory, his movement no longer modifies my perceptions, determines my responses. I do not adjust, accommodate, or adapt; I resist. The weight and heat of the extended arm are present but not primary; muffled and diluted by other stimuli, they exist only on the periphery, at the outer limit of consciousness.)

In the darkness, interior and exterior converge. The walls of the cabin (formerly defined by light and

27

reflection, by an exclusively visual symmetry) no longer separate an arbitrary quadrate of space from the forest. Instead, they become huge tympanic membranes, diaphragmatic partitions that transmit and amplify (by periodic vibration) the soft scrapings of nocturnal insects, the muted flight of large frugivorous bats.

The sounds are intensified, received at several times their normal volume. Lying flat on my back, buoyed up by the canvass, I hear (or imagine I can hear) large hard-winged beetles crawling across Heliconia leaves, the soft sucking sound of a hawk moth probing the elongated calyx of an epiphytic lily, the steady shock of falling water.

Patterns emerge, persistent sonic categories. I postulate an invisible topography: Large cold flowers with petals the consistency of flesh hang motionless over the water; particles of pollen (dislodged from the lips, colorless, silent) drifting out over the concealed surface.

Mark moves again, pushing up against me.

Kirsten is crawling through a small tunnel in the cave, moving on her stomach through several inches of water. The tunnel curves downhill, bending to the left. As Kirsten pushes forward, it grows more narrow; the roof slants toward the floor; the walls press in along the sides of her body. Above her (suspended in a dense, impenetrable layer) there is 250 feet of solid limestone.

Kirsten pulls herself along on her elbows and knees, pushing with the toes of her boots, drawing her arms in closed to her sides. Twisting her shoulders, she slides across the uneven floor of the tunnel, lowering her head to avoid outcroppings of rock. As she lifts it, her headlamp seems to grow dinner, to tremble slightly. The shadows on the opposite wall become less distinct; the outlines are lost, the contours blurred. They seem to have been projected through a piece of cheesecloth, thrown on the surface of the rock through a coarse scrim.

The water becomes deeper. Kirsten moves through it mechanically, never changing the rhythm of her progress. Rising up over the lower portion of her body, the water covers her chest and the tip of her chin. Kirsten (still moving forward) turns her head sideways, holding the flame of her lamp well above the surface, pressing her cheek against the roof.

Kirsten stops and detaches her headband. Only her head, her hand, and her wrist are visible. The rest of her body has disappeared beneath the water. Kirsten works slowly, deliberately, as if encountering great resistance. She unclasps her headband with intense concentration, as though planning the motion of each finger, coordinating a number of complex positions, pressures, tensions, and directions.

Holding the lamp in one hand (palms open, fingers curved around the base of the reflector), Kirsten shines the light ahead of her, tilting the beam slightly downhill. The light does not penetrate the water, does not reveal the hidden portions of her body, the bottom of the tunnel. A few feet away, the roof slants down until it is less than an inch from the surface of the water. A cold breeze blows through the hole, escaping from the interior of the cave as if under pressure. The water itself is motionless; there are no currents, no perturbations. It stretches out in front of Kirsten like a strip of black glass, reflecting back the light in a bright, steady band.

Replacing her headlamp, Kirsten reaches out and grabs both sides of the tunnel. Then she lowers her head and pushes her face below the surface. The light goes out. Kirsten begins to swim downhill, pulling herself along underwater across the uneven floor of the tunnel. There is a faint splashing sound. Complete darkness.

♦ ♦ ♦

Mark blows out the match. As the light from the lamp spreads across the table, shadows begin to radiate from the center like the spokes in a wheel. Kirsten's face suddenly appears, perfectly distinct, suspended over the surface, every detail exposed and expanded. The light moves into the corners of the room, penetrating various objects, reflected by others according to their density and opacity. It expands in regular waves, passing through the strands of a black mist net, projecting onto the opposite wall a web several times larger than the original, a sequence of regular lines and flat yellow squares.

As it continues to fill the cabin, the light is reflected from rolls of chicken wire, metal traps, and curved steel cages. It bounces off a row of empty brown bottles, off the flat, bright heads of a dozen new nails. This reflected light, diminished in intensity, fills the room a second time, passing through the cords of a hemp hammock, between the threads of the white sheet which hangs down from the center of the cabin. Almost extinguished, it reaches the distant corners of the cabin, filtering through the slats of a broken orange crate, drifting onto high shelves in small, dust-like particles. Finally, moving as if under pressure, the light escapes through thousands of tiny chinks, flowing out into the forest, pushing back the peripheral shadows.

At the same time, the cabin turns another degree away from the sun, and the air, cooled slightly, moves into different currents, new configurations. As the air changes in temperature and pressure, a flock of parrots—invisible at the edge of the forest—begins to produce a series of sharp, attenuated cries which mix dissonantly with the low, triadic call-notes of a distant Tonami. Beneath the voices of the birds, running in a kind of atonal counterpoint, the high-pitched vibrations of various species of frogs can be heard; the dry scraping of nocturnal insects; the faint, intermittent sounds of arboreal snakes sliding over damp leaves.

The noises suddenly stop. Despite their apparent randomness, they seem to have accomplished some sort of purpose—perhaps generated a system or established a tenuous hierarchy. Almost immediately, the sounds inside the cabin increase in volume as if amplified several times. The muffled clink of a knife blade against a tin plate, the irregular breathing of the two people, the creaking of the chairs, and the hissing of the kerosene lamp blend into a kind of static, become a band of white noise broadcast into the silent forest.

♦ ♦ ♦

As Eduardo bends forward, frozen over the moving blade, his sister reappears behind him, floating to the surface of the pool—face down, arms flung out to either side. Her body is limp, relaxed, moving with the current. As Dulce-Maria drifts out of the sunlight, she seems to merge with the water, to become vague, indistinct, dissolving around the edges like a crystal of salt. Her arms enter the shadows first, passing into solution, becoming part of a substance without structure, without separate parts. Her back (wet, shining, covered by the same streaks of light that are reflected from the surface of the pool) blends into the water as though she has suddenly assumed a protective coloration, changed her skin like a chameleon (without effort, by instinct) to mimic her background.

Dulce-Maria drifts towards the far end of the pool. As she passes under the trees, shadows (overhanging branches, leaves, vines, epiphytes, mirrored by the surface, interrupted momentarily by the passing body, modified and distorted) move down her spine like a procession of ants. Her back and buttocks are tattooed with pale blue lozenges, with a net of fine black bands (twig and stem projected onto the floating form, thrown onto her body) that stretches from her neck to her heels.

Dulce-Maria drifts back into the sunlight. The contours of her body become more distinct, more definite. She moves both arms simultaneously, pulling them in to her sides, pushing herself forward through the water. The girl draws her legs together, reducing herself to a perfect cylinder, to a surface rotated around a single axis. Slick, buoyant, slender, she drifts downstream like a small balsa tree, her heavy hair floating out behind like a mass of wet, black roots.

Eduardo continues to move the blade of his machete in slow, steady circles. Opening his mouth slightly, he exhales a puff of smoke, clamping the damp end of the cigarette between his teeth. The smoke rises straight up, bends, blows out over the pool, and disappears into the shadows.

Suddenly the girl dives. Only the soles of her feet can be seen moving beneath the surface of the water. She hands suspended for a moment, then vanishes with a kick that sends the water into a series of overlapping circles, into a sequence of concentric waves that move out towards the edge of the pool.

The boy stands up, throws down his machete, and dives in after her.

◆ ◆ ◆

As Eduardo enters the water (breaking up the images on the surface, interrupting and distorting the oval of reflected sunlight) his body seems to bend at a right angle, to be deflected slightly, refracted and modified. Patches of yellow skin (behind the neck, around the waist, along the backs of the legs, across the soles of his feet) expand, blend together, covering the moving form with a thin, translucent sheath, a hard flexible chitin.

Kicking his feet, Eduardo swims towards the far end of the pool. On the surface of the rock (just behind him, slightly to the left) spots of water begin to dry, shrinking at the edges, leaving small damp rings on the blade and handle of the machete.

Far below the surface, on the opposite side of the pool, the two children can be seen swimming in and out of the sunken snags, moving between the heavy, wet limbs, trees, roots, underwater plants. They push their way forward, arms stretched out in front of them, palms open, fingers spread, feeling their way along the bottom like blind, albino fish.

Almost simultaneously, the two surface. Treading water, suspended at the center of the pool, Dulce-Maria holds a small, green lizard between her teeth. The animal (mottled, colored like the sunken snags) lies motionless, limp, its tail trailing in the water. Her brother swims towards the bank, using only one hand. In the other he holds a large, black water snake.

(The snake twists back on itself, winding its body around the boy's arm, coiling around his neck and chin. Eduardo continues to swim slowly, holding the animal firmly behind the head with his thumb and first two fingers. The snake opens its mouth; blindly, rhythmically, it moves from side to side, striking at shadows, lunging at an invisible target. Its body (long, wet, shining) reflects the sunlight like a strip of polished coal.)

Grabbing the lizard by its hind feet, Dulce-Maria tosses it up on the shore. As the scales dry, they begin to turn a dull shade of brown, mimicking the color and texture of the surrounding rocks.

Dulce-Maria turns and swims back to the opposite end of the pool.

Without climbing out of the water, Eduardo reaches up and grabs his machete. Still holding the snake behind the head, he wrenches the body off his arm, slaps it out flat on the bank, and cuts it in half, tossing the pieces to the left of the drying lizard.

(Both halves twist convulsively for a moment, then stop. The two animals lie side by side without moving.)

Pulling himself out of the water with both hands, Eduardo shakes himself like a wet dog and bends down. Leaning forward, he picks up the smoldering cigarette and clamps it between his teeth. Then, stooping over again, he tears up a handful of grass, wipes off the blade of his machete, and begins to sharpen it, pulling it across the rock in slow, steady circles.

(Kirsten steps farther back into the shadows, unties her blue and white kerchief, and mops the sweat from her forehead and chest. Then, turning her back on the pool, she walks silently upstream in the direction of the bridge.)

Dulce-Maria rolls over, folds her hands behind her head, and floats on her back. Her body is sustained by the water, partially suspended on the surface.

◆ ◆ ◆

I move forward mechanically, swimming downhill, pulling myself along underwater over the uneven floor of the tunnel. I am no longer able to determine the exact position of my body, no longer capable of imagining its motion relative to any fixed point.

The cave closes in on me—a thick, invisible curve, hydrolytic, homogenous, solvent. Time and space are replaced by an indefinite protraction, a steady, sequential extension. I am caught in a single action infinitely repeated, a blind, kinesthetic reflex.

(Lifting one hand, Kirsten pushes herself around a slight bend in the passage. A rock scrapes across her wrist, tearing the cuff of her shirt. No sensation, nothing. The water is cold, anesthetic. Kirsten reaches out again, following the rough edge of the rock with the tip of one finger, trying to create (tactually, by texture) a nonvisual map of her surroundings. She rubs one hand along the wall abrasively, as if attempting to separate herself from her environment, to orient herself by the coordinates of pain and pressure. Nothing. The palm of her hand is numb, unresponsive.)

I twist my shoulders, forcing my way through the narrow, curving tunnel. I can distinguish my body from the water only by slight differences in temperature, structure, and density. I am limited almost entirely to subjective perceptions—to visceral feedback, to the internal tensions of muscles, tendons, and joints.

(Kirsten lifts one hand. There is no space between the roof and the surface of the water, no air pocket above her head. Reaching out to both sides (elbows locked, arms drawn in close) she attempts to push herself backwards, to swim uphill out of the tunnel. Her motions are slow, methodical, systematic, a chain of instinctive patterns directed towards no conscious goal. She seems to react automatically, with a certain indifference.)

(As she approaches the bend, her hips become tightly wedged between two walls. Kirsten pushes out into the darkness, rocking her body back and forth, twisting her shoulders, as if by these random, undirected motions she could force herself back through the opening. Her struggle is invisible; it takes place in absolute silence—diffused, osmotic, immediately assimilated.)

Mark breaks off a three-inch piece of twine and ties it around both legs. Adding the humming bird to the bottom of the string, he moves back to the table and picks up another specimen.

He leans forward. The only sound is the scraping of his chair, the steady hiss of the lamp. Making a longitudinal incision in the abdomen, Mark begins to detach the skin, methodically, cutting the connective tissue with the tip of his scalpel.

(The birds have been hung up to dry like a string of peppers. Threaded on a piece of nylon fish line, they move back and forth above the surface of the cot, rotating around a central axis. In the semi-darkness, the bodies blend together, forming an elongated cone of blue, green, brown, and black feathers; a diminishing spiral interrupted by smaller cones, by red and yellow beaks, the orange tips of dried claws.)

As marks leans forward into the light, his pupils contract. His eyes (reflecting the flame of the lamp) seem to empty automatically.

♦ ♦ ♦

Dulce-Maria's eye dilate rapidly. As if coming from a great distance, the pupils expand, filling the iris, rising towards the surface from an indefinite depth.

(Conjunctiva, cornea, sclerotic, chorioid, ciliary muscle, ciliary process, iris, suspensory ligament, posterior aqueous chamber, lens, vitreous humor, retina, optic nerve. The eye responds, changing reflexively.)

On the surface (as if projected on a curved, plastic screen), the interior of the cabin is reproduced in miniature, reflected into two convex mirrors, divided on the corneas into identical images. These images (confined to the two ovals, moving with them) expand out from the center as the pupils dilate.

Dulce-Maria turns her head as if watching a moving object. As she turns, the door frame bends, following the curve of the cornea, passing across the iris like a floating branch. Moving with the frame, the nylon screen (each square compressed slightly, shrinking as it approaches the corner of the eye) curves forward, disappearing into the whites. The screen (reproduced in miniature) becomes a green filter, a horizontal lid that closes over the iris, straining it into thousands of identical segments.

The mosaic is repeated. Each of the individual pieces is holographically perfect; each mimics the proportions and positions of real objects, arranging them in a space that seems to generate its own depth.

As Dulce-Maria turns her head, the interior of the cabin is copied onto her cornea, transferred to a moving graph which reduces the relative relationships to points within an n-dimensional matrix. Foreground and background appear; a vanishing point is established.

Beneath the reflections, the girl's eyes contain only their own structure—conjunctiva, cornea, sclerotic.

♦ ♦ ♦

Kirsten is wedged between the walls of the tunnel. Reaching out to both sides, she tries to push herself backwards, to swim to the surface. Her fingers (numb, invisible, moving without conscious control) sink into a layer of cold, sticky mud. They bend slightly, scooping up handful after handful of wet gravel, digging down in search of a firm substratum. The mud seems bottomless, unstable, infinite.

Kirsten loses all sense of direction. She can no longer tell if she is moving forward or backward, up or down. She is detached from her actions, watching them from a great distance without interest or curiosity, as if, floating freely, she need no longer concern herself with the ordinary categories of space and time. Her fingers move, bending slightly, pushing against the sides of the tunnel. They seem to belong to someone else.

(Underwater, in complete darkness, the eyes begin to generate their own light. Spots of blue and gray (abstract, formless, surrounded by bright white coronas that rotate around the rims) seem to move into the foreground from a great distance, expanding until they merge into a flat, luminescent surface that fills the entire visual field. Streaks of orange and red light move across the surface in slow, asymmetrical coils, breaking it up into hundreds of narrow fissures. From time to time there is an intense flash, a burst of mercury oxide that moves out from the center like a nova, consuming all other colors, disappearing suddenly into the darkness. The spots of blue and gray come forward again, moving up from a great distance.)

Digging the toes of her boots into the gravel, Kirsten pushes herself backwards, freeing her hips from the walls of the tunnel. She floats slowly up, out of the water, breaking the surface. Kirsten opens her mouth and takes a deep breath. There is no visual difference between the air and the water, only tactile variations in temperature, density, and texture. The boundary between the two elements is invisible, the darkness uniform, uninterrupted. Without turning around, Kirsten begins to crawl back towards the mouth of the tunnel.

◆ ◆ ◆

Kirsten leans over the table. She feels (unconsciously) the body heat of the man beside her, the shallow currents of his breathing, the minute relocations, extensions, and contractions of his muscles and her own. To a lesser degree, she also perceives (again subliminally) the movements, growths, and accommodations of the living things outside the cabin.

As if made restless by these sensations, Kirsten moves, turning her body along a perpendicular axis until her eyes are parallel to the center of the window. Simultaneously, she rubs her hand (palm flat, fingers together, extended) across her face, detaching small, flattened drops of water, globes of sweat which break, spread, and evaporate.

Completing the semi-circle (the side of her face now turned towards the window, her eyes on a level with those of the man), Kirsten moves her lips, speaking in a low, quick voice. Mark, responding to her words, rises slowly, lifting his body out of the chair, swelling, expanding, as though he were being pumped full of helium. He raises one arm, and his left hand moves in and out of the circle of light like a large, translucent moth.

Reaching out over the rungs of her chair, Kirsten bends down, unties her boots, and sticks the cuffs of her pants into the tops. Then, using both hands, she pushes the laces back through the metal eyes, winding the extra pieces of cord twice around her ankles and securing them with a square knot. Getting up, she walks in the direction of the door. As she passes the orange crate, she moves her hands over the top, picking up a small, three-ring notebook; two yellow pencils; a pair of steel forceps; a pistol (loaded with dust-shot), and several plastic bottles. In each bottle a small circle of yellow blotting paper, a lump of damp cotton, and a shallow layer of white cyanide crystals are visible. In one, some of the crystals have melted and are sticking to the sides and bottom. Tightening the tops of the containers, Kirsten sticks them into the right hand pocket of her work shirt, buttoning down the flap with her thumb and index finger.

Without turning his head, Mark says something. On the table in front of him, there are now two dead birds, a large frugivorous bat, a canvas bag, and a jar filed with a light green liquid. The jar contains formaldehyde.

Kirsten bends over and picks up an aluminum rod, a circle of stiff wire, and a small white net bag. As she straightens up, she reaches out and picks up a battery-operated headlamp attacked to a black elastic band. Slipping the band over her blue and white bandanna, Kirsten begins to assemble the insect net, pulling the net bag onto the wire circle, screwing the tip of the handle clockwise into the threads. When the net is completed, she moves rapidly towards the door, crossing the threshold, disappearing suddenly, submerging herself in the darkness, assimilated by it.

♦ ♦ ♦

Outside of the cabin, the forest emerges slowly, precipitating as a series of reflections, recreated at the intersection of air and water, condensing along the elemental interface.

About two hundred yards above the bridge, slightly to the left of the main bank, a small creek empties into the river forming a shallow triangle of gravel and twigs. At the mouth of the creek, a long vine hangs out over the water, projected onto the river (as if on a screen), foreshortened as it recedes from the surface, compressed, reduced, and distorted.

The vine hangs rigidly at right angles to the major plane, perfectly perpendicular. Along the cable, broad heart-shaped leaves are twisted out, turned to expose the pale green undersides, the soft pliable venation of the vascular tissue. Seen from above, the leaves appear opaque, pointed, crossed by a system of small ridges that radiate out in a semicircle from the stem, shallow ripples, expanding systematically from a single point. Repeated in the water, reduced to two dimensions, these veins appear to curve, to coil back on themselves, long hollow tubes symmetrically arranged around a central axis.

Although the vine itself is motionless, the reflection seems to move, to waver slightly, oscillating from side to side as if it were suspended in a column of heat, a clear, ascending current. Interrupted by floating sticks and grass, the image breaks apart, dissolving at the edges, stretching and contracting, floating downstream into the shadows. At other times, it seems to penetrate the surface, to coat the bottom with a stream of transparent images.

Occasionally the patterns are interrupted by something moving across them—by a large black fish swimming in and out between the sunken snags. As the

46

fish passes beneath the vine, the river is momentarily split in half, divided into two separate screens. Most of the reflections remain static, floating like an oily film on the surface of the water. Others are transferred to the fish. Crossing the blunt head, moving along the dorsal fins, they conform to the body, flowing with it, disappearing, cut off by the tail fin. A piece of the vine is detached, severed from the central tube; floating across the scales, it appears as a colored emulsion.

Suddenly the perspective changes. The reflections stop and the fish begins to move. Swimming downstream slowly, passing silently through the dark, cool water, the fish drifts through the images like a person walking in front of a slide projector. Twisting his body, changing the angle and intensity of the light, he covers himself with scraps of sky, pieces of vines, bits of leaf, a semi-transparent mosaic, kaleidoscopic, fragmental.

For an instant, the fish and the reflections seems to merge into a single category, monadic, an organism without segments, parts, or divisions. Then they separate. The animal moves off into the shadows, swimming below a colorless surface.

♦ ♦ ♦

Mark turns slowly, pressing up against me, pushing towards the edge of the cot. He progresses at a steady rate, thermotropically, with a blind, amoebic insistence, as if trying (even in his sleep) to envelop and assimilate my body. As he moves across the bed, I experience him as a pure force, a colloidal pressure: hot intrusive, alien.

(I open my eyes, but the dream continues. I am wedged between the walls of the tunnel, trapped underwater. Reaching out to both sides, I try to push myself backwards, to swim up to the surface. My fingers (detached, invisible, moving without conscious control) sink into a layer of warm mud. They bend slightly, scooping up handful after handful of wet gravel. The mud seems bottomless, unstable, infinite. It moves towards me in a dense, solid mass, forcing me against the opposite wall.)

Mark coughs and throws his left arm across my chest. I resist automatically.

(Digging the toes of my boots into the gravel, I push myself backwards, freeing my hips and shoulders from the walls of the tunnel. I float up slowly, drifting with the current, breaking the surface without a ripple. Turning over on my back, I open my mouth and take a long, deep breath.)

48

◆ ◆ ◆

Kirsten's body is covered with a pelt of bubbles; a coat of fine, transparent hairs composed of small, colorless globes of air. The globes are strung together, flattened at the top and bottom, as if attached by an invisible adhesive. They rise slowly, breaking through the surface, creating at regular intervals an extensive system of overlapping ripples.

Kirsten opens her mouth and exhales. Larger bubbles drift out of her throat, emerge from her nostrils in two symmetrical streams. Each is separate, distinct, a perfect sphere that floats through the water like a hollow glass ball, expanding and breaking at the surface. Seen from below, the bubbles appear to disappear, as if, rising in a continuous chain, they suddenly had been absorbed into another medium, as if they had passed (by force of diffusion) through a liquid membrane.

Looking up, Kirsten can see large spots of light moving across the surface, expanding and contracting like pieces of living protoplasm. Filtered through the overhanging trees, the shifting light gives the illusion that a flotilla of jellyfish is crossing the pool; the beams the penetrate the water (floating out from the spots at an acute angle, refracted, incomplete) look like long, elastic tentacles. Kirsten allows herself to drift upwards, holding herself flat, parallel to the bottom of the pool. Drawing her arms to her sides, she moves her hands in a series of rapid sculling motions, as if attempting to maintain an even, continuous velocity.

The water becomes warmer. A blurred reflection of the sky (an intense, flat sheet of blue interrupted by irregular ivory splotches) is projected onto the underside of the surface. Trees appear, distorted, curved out over the water, hanging in a volume that has no depth. Foreground and background merge, reducing height to width, proximity to intensity. Leaves and branches appear to move discontinuously, as if pressed behind several layers of thick glass, permitted only gross alterations in arrangement and position.

Kirsten turns her head. The water pushes against her eardrums, producing a constant, muffled roar, a single sustained tone that rises in pitch as she approaches the surface.

As it rises, the floating body appears to swell, to become brighter, more distinct. A face appears, surrounded by a semicircle of tangled hair. Kirsten lifts her shoulders out of the water, condensing slowly at the center of the pool, precipitating out of the solution. Rolling over on her back, she floats like a radial spoke, moving clockwise, arms spread out to either side, eyes closed, head back. The water on her body evaporates in an invisible stream; her face, chest, and the tops of her legs dry rapidly. As her breasts grow warmer, the nipples relax, blending into the areolae.

Kirsten lies limply on the surface, moving with the current.

◆ ◆ ◆

The walls dissolve, and the forest enters the cabin.

Lying on my back, I see (suspended above me) a cluster of objects moving randomly, falling towards my face in slow motion. Only partially condensed, they drift across my field of vision like splotches of reflected light, coenesthetic, without conformation or direction.

Mark turns in his sleep, pressing up against me. I move away, sliding across the cot, disentangled, dilated, extended into the darkness.

The objects precipitate. I watch the outlines become more distinct, precise, definitive. The centers expand slowly, taking on substance and detail, assuming fixed, definite forms, systematic crystalloid patterns. Reaching out to both sides, I find myself surrounded by a net of transparent lianas, thick colorless leaves, masses of small, clear-winged butterflies.

Suddenly (without being able to trace the source of the sensation), I feel that I have crossed a boundary, have entered a complex, balanced system, a web of reciprocal contacts, geodesic, pervasive, contingent at no single point. Moving slowly through the drifting vegetation (through a long series of coherent hallucinations), I find that I can no longer separate myself from the forest, differentiate and isolate my body. The objects (observed or dreamed, visible, intangible) have absorbed me, have reproduced (macroscopically) the ontogeny of my consciousness.

(Turning in his sleep, Mark is integrated into the system, absorbed and subsumed. His influence—the slow, amoebic insistence of his body—is diluted, titrated, neutralized. I feel his dissolution and am released.)

The forest continues to congeal, without any specific sexuality, without men, without maleness,

51

polymorphic, sustained by internal conjugation, by the simultaneous union of all parts. Lianas condense into spiremes and are held in permanent prophase; karyokinetic patterns emerge; the walls of the cabin dissolve completely; mitosis is arrested.

◆ ◆ ◆

The path bisects the clearing. Running through the center, it divides the open space into two equal segments, into mirror images mutually reflecting. On either side of the line (a narrow band of bent grasses which passes invisibly through the center of the cabin), there is a kind of bilateral symmetry; a correspondence of species, colors, positions, and densities; an almost perfect reciprocity. Only the forest (appearing along the edges of the circle as a band of peripheral intrusions) interrupts the illusion of congruence, blurring and distorting the borders like the rim of a warped mirror.

Superimposed on this primary form, there is a secondary pattern. A number of faint depressions run discontinuously across the clearing, filling both halves of the circle with a network of broken lines. These lines intersect the main path at various angles, run parallel to it, reverse their direction, depth, and width at random intervals. Created by the sporadic movements of small mammals, generated from the incomplete tracks of leafcutter ants and the trails of snakes and lizards, this secondary pattern is less stable, less persistent. Reestablished each day under different conditions, its form is fluid, mobile, undefined.

Time-lapse photography reveals a kind of Brownian movement of discrete lines, a perpetual, random oscillation. Under such conditions, the cabin appears to be caught at the center of an immense, moving web; enmeshed in a pattern of shadows which changed with each fluctuation in the angle and intensity of light.

♦ ♦ ♦

Compression.

The air, cooling slightly, becomes dense, solvent, partially opaque. As the light decreases, details disappear, gradually merging to form large, compact masses—shapes without content, surfaces without depth. Moving into the same plane, objects (reduced to indistinct silhouettes) expand, creating (by a kind of mutual extension) a uniform, two-dimensional surface. As if duplicating this process in a different medium, the individual sounds of the forest contract into a single, sustained tone.

The picture is overdeveloped.

Caught in the shadow of the forest, the cabin blends into the trees—a dark, flat rectangle that dilates slowly, filling the interstices between the trunks; almost simultaneously, the path begins to spread out to either side, covering the clearing with a thin, viscous emulsion that shifts slowly from gray to black.

On the other side of the hill (invisible, unobserved), the river rises above its banks; fused with the bridge, it forms an elemental bond, a single, organic particle.

Earth, air, water. The final synthesis takes place in total darkness, silently, by degrees.

◆ ◆ ◆

Kirsten stops in the center of the bridge and switches off her headlamp. Moving slowly through the darkness, she drags the palm of her hand along the upper surface of the rail. The only noise is the sound of running water.

From the bridge, the opposite bank appears to be a flat gray wall splattered with dark blotches. The wall is one-dimensional, without depth or texture. The blotches (perhaps fallen logs or the trunks of large trees) point in all directions with no particular orientation in space, as though, suspended in some sort of fluid, they have become independent from any gravitational tropism. The vertical and horizontal planes of vision have merged so completely that it is impossible to tell what is growing up (moving away from the ground, stretching towards the canopy) and what has fallen sideways (across the forest floor). All the vegetation appears to have been distributed randomly through the available space.

Kirsten moves forward, treading down wave after wave of warm, invisible air. The lower portion of her body blends into the shadows. Only her face and arms are visible, pale, disembodied. As she enters the forest on the opposite side of the river, they seem to float down from a great height, to swim (independently, as though not connected to a central axis) to the bottom of a deep pool.

Kirsten pushes her way through the dense brush. Her arms appear and disappear, moving in and out between the shadows. It is as though her body is being carried through the forest by an invisible current, buoyed up on a raft of tangled vegetation. Occasionally a liana brushes against her cheek, drifting down from the canopy like a strand of black kelp. Aerial roots become the tentacles of minute coelenterates, of whole flotillas of transparent jellyfish.

Without switching on her headlamp, Kirsten begins to move downstream towards the pool.

◆ ◆ ◆

I turn slightly, shifting my weight, pressing my head and shoulders back against the cot. As I move, the forest moves with me, erasing all fixed points of reference. I retain only a subliminal perception of my position, a vague kinesthetic orientation.

(Linked together sequentially, the images generate an associative taxonomy, a strict chain of congruences linked together by logical transformations. Mark reaches out to adjust the lamp; a stick floats downstream, drifting towards the center of the pool. As he leans forward, his bare elbow becomes the curve of Eduardo's shoulder, the sharp circular pattern of a moving machete. Just above the bridge, a Heliconia leaf follows the sun, turning in a long, steady semicircle from east to west, exposing a slick, curved surface; Eduardo moves through the light, reflecting it. Mark closes his eyes, covering the corneas; the eyelids are wrinkled slightly; gathered together in fine, overlapping folds. I see (without transition) tightly rolled bracts, diascoraceae, cones, spiraled leaves, a large yellow-billed toucan, aesclepidaceae, columns of petals, milk, mist nets, orange aphids, hair, Spanish moss, chusquea, grass, bamboo, Eduardo's fingers, my hands, whorls, fused petals, concentric veins, a coiled bothrops, hands of braided sisal, ridges of dust; bands of reflected light, running down the margins of leaves, distorting them with illusory motion—acerose, linear, lanceolate, elliptic, ensiform, oblong, oblanceolate, ovate, cordate (ascending curve, point, constant rhythm; the movement of Eduardo's blood, the diastolic contractions of his body), reniform, orbiculate (shoulder, underarm, indented stem) runciate, lyrate, peltate.

In front of me, the forest moves like a strip of film, a continuous diaphanous band of colored images. Superimposed on it, another set of events is being projected simultaneously. The two streams (memory and hallucination) run independently, at different speeds, generating (as they pass over each other) a series of double exposures. There is a temporary convergence of cause and effect, a transposition of past and present. At some unspecified instant, simultaneity is established; the two reels are synchronized.

(Eduardo appears at the point of intersection. I see him clearly, without distortion.)

◆ ◆ ◆

Eduardo. In whom I did not recognize the
catalyst of my transformation, the mutative impetus;
who appeared to me as an isolated fragment, alien,
inaccessible, an initial E without consection or
continuation. Eduardo. The blind instant of transition,
whom I possessed automatically (without knowledge of
that possession) as the culmination of an uninitiated
process. Eduardo. First seen (from the air) as a single
point (colorless, motile, embryonic), perceived as a
moving body, a flagellate particle, gametic, involuntary,
incomplete.

(We come in high over the clearing and circle
around to the south. Below us the workers' quarters
(two peeled sticks placed parallel at the center of a ring
of red clay) revolve slowly, turning as we turn in a wide,
steady circle, the radial spokes of a revolving wheel. To
the left, another strip of dirt leads downhill towards the
river, passing (as an imaginary line, disconnected,
momentarily suspended) through the cabin and ending
abruptly at the far edge of the clearing. On the other
side of the forest (as if perpetuating the potential
trajectory of the path) a log bridge stretches across the
river. Several hundred yards downstream, a large pool
appears, partially covered by overhanging trees. The
clearing is empty. Nothing is moving.)

(We circle again, coming in lower for the final
approach. Suddenly (beneath us, crossing the shadow of
the descending plane) two white dots emerge from one
of the houses and begin to move towards the center of
the clearing. Lifting the tip of the left wing, the pilot
banks sharply, throwing me up against Mark. I feel him
move away towards the opposite side of the cockpit.
Almost simultaneously, the horizon (detached by the
eccentric pattern of our approach) rises up solidly in
front of the windshield, tilting the clearing like an

59

empty plate; the two dots (colorless, motile, embryonic) move towards the bottom rim, opaque drops sliding down an inclined plane.)

(The wheels touch the landing strip. Leaning forward, I can see a segment of the forest through the window. The trees are periodically interrupted, distorted by the invisible blades of the propeller; they move from side to side, translucent strands of kelp drifting in an invisible current, giant underwater plants anchored to the bottom by colorless prop roots. As the motor stops, the scene slowly congeals, crystallizing in from the edges.)

(I close my eyes slightly. The windshield (curving around me on all three sides) becomes a prism, a lens that magnifies and refracts the light, filling the inside of the cockpit with long, incandescent blue bands, cylindrical filaments that flicker in the heat. Outside, the sun (directly overhead) gives the clearing an overexposed quality. Everything looks flat, white, slightly faded.)

(Complete silence. I reach down and unfasten my seatbelt with a metallic click. As I lift my head, Eduardo and his sister appear at the far edge of the landing strip.)

♦ ♦ ♦

Lines become fluid, unsteady, indefinite. Reflections flow back to their source. The trunks of trees dissolve, drift in towards the banks of the river. the leaves—stretched and distorted by the moving water— pass along their own stems, moving up the overhanging branches, blending with the bark, changing their shape, texture, and color.

The boy sits motionless, bent forward, staring at the reflections. The surface of the pool appears to be covered with huge amoebae, with masses of luminescent protoplasm that expand at a constant rate, dividing into mirror images of one another. Eduardo watches the bright splotches of light move across the water. Half closing his eyes, he blends them into one immense organism.

The movement stops; the pseudopods are retracted. Now the surface of the pool seems to be covered with a flat, even veneer, a golden liquid without boundary or depth. Particles of light hang in suspension, suffused through the water.

Eduardo turns his head to the left, lowering his chin slightly. A face appears, floating up from the depths of the reflection to the surface. It appears from behind, as though projected through a scrim.

Eduardo does not move. He sits in the same position, bent forward from the waist, watching the floating face drift closer, grow larger, bland, disembodied, almost hidden behind three huge bell-shaped flowers.

A hand appears. Motion begins. It continues in a descending parabola, asymptotic, leveling into an infinite extension, an arc which approaches but never intersects the absissa. Eduardo watches the hand move across the surface of the water.

♦ ♦ ♦

I reach out and push aside the Datura flowers.

(A kind of consistent clearness suspends my mind just above the surface of the action, a barrier of green glass, thin, translucent, curving out infinitely in all directions. My arms (floating out from my body) dissolve and penetrate the barrier (a sheet of heat and reflected light), moving through it in two symmetrical arcs. I feel the rough surface of the leaves brush across my hands and wrists, the cool blurred texture of overlapping stems. Turning slowly, the flowers seems to drift out over the surface of the water; five fused tubular anthers; five symmetrical petals.)

(On the other side of the glass (pushing it out, bending it towards me) there appears to be a heavy, colorless liquid. Everything beyond the flowers is indistinct, out of focus. From time to time, a form breaks through the surface leaving a trail of large, flat bubbles. The bubbles rise gradually, spinning slightly, moving through the fluid as though they were being squeezed out of a clear plastic tube. They pass in front of me, hollow, iridescent lenses that magnify and distort the tips of my fingers.)

I close my eyes. The act is arrested, reduced to a hypothesis, a movement (remembered, unrealized) that seems to have taken place underwater. Events move more slowly through this medium, pushing forward through a sticky, viscid resin. The past is expanded, dilated, extended through time. My hand begins to move. Every portion of the action, each arc of change and angle of descent is drawn out interminably. My hand floats towards an object—a leaf, a cup, a bit of grass. It moves in slow motion, forcing its way through the liquid with difficulty. There is no completion, no consummation. The frames are infinite. I move towards

Eduardo blindly, unconsciously, without postulating the end of my motion.

(My hand continues to move, as if treading water, without reaching its goal. I contemplate it from a great distance, detached, disengaged. The action (remembered, unrealized) appears to have no consequences; nothing connects; nothing touches; there are no relationships established. My hand continues to move, turning slowly, drifting away from my body. It floats across an expanding distance, stretching out towards a receding point, isolated, disconnected, hermetically sealed in its own trajectory.)

(Each segment of the action seems to exist in a perpetual present, without cause, without effect, cataleptically arrested at one instant in time. The motion of my hand (perceived in memory as a line of static events) can only be completed artificially, can only be concluded by a shift in perspective, a radical refocusing.)

I close my eyes, forcing the object to occupy the center of my visual field. To the left, something is still moving, still coming into existence, materializing out of a vacuum. For a moment, I am caught between the object and the action. I force myself to ignore the peripheral movement, the slowly descending hand. Suddenly the object grows larger, takes on depth, texture, color, and form. I see (hanging in front of me, motionless, suspended in empty space) a large, white, bell-shaped flower. A hand appears simultaneously, static, immobile; the fingers are curled tightly around the lower portion of the stem. (In another frame, the hand is still approaching; here it has already arrived. The action (complete and incomplete, remembered and realized) exists in two forms, in two concurrent positions.)

As if arranging snapshots in chronological order, I proceed to infer a sequence, to establish a probable chain of events. By moving the static memories rapidly, I generate the illusion of motion.

I open my eyes. Eduardo is sitting in front of me, partially screened by the Datura bush. I reach out and push aside the flowers. The arc (sustained, luminous, incandescent) is completed.

♦ ♦ ♦

Moving as slowly as possible, Kirsten reaches between the leaves.

At the far edge of the pool, several hummingbirds are hovering around the Heliconia. Their wings move rapidly, distorting the outline of their bodies, reducing them to iridescent strips, prismatic bands that move rapidly from flower to flower.

Eduardo leans forward, watching the birds. From time to time, he picks up a small pebble, holds it just above the water, and releases it. The pebbles hesitate for a moment, suspended in empty space, then disappear, sucked to the bottom of the pool. Eduardo leans farther forward, watching them shrink, blending into the shadows along the bottom. As each pebble falls, it leaves a distinct trail of small, flat bubbles, transparent globes that rise slowly to the surface.

Kirsten parts the bush, pushing it to one side. The enormous bell-shaped flowers of the Datura move slightly, scattering minute flecks of pollen in a long floating spiral, a particulate line of yellow dust that drifts out towards the center of the pool. The water is coated with a thin, fine-grained film.

Eduardo picks up another pebble. As he reaches out over the surface, his thumb and first three fingers are met by their own reflection. For a moment, a huge pink spider seems to be walking upside down across a piece of glass, swimming half-submerged across the pool. The fifth finger, curled to one side, distorted and elongated by the moving water (by the impact of the falling pebble, by the regular currents of the river) appears as a strand of silk, a bit of web floating out from the body of the spider. Caught from another angle, rotated by a twist of the wrist, this same finger seems to curl back on itself, retracted and coiled like the tongue of a hawk moth. Seen from behind, it is an indistinct shadow, a moving strip of sepia.

Eduardo withdraws his hand. The water is motionless again, a cold, clear oval of polished quartz, perfect, uniform, without a chip or scratch.

Kirsten reaches out again. A small brown ant is crawling around the stem of one of the Datura flowers, working its way steadily towards the other side. As if responding to an invisible signal, it turns suddenly and begins to move down the lip, following the seam of two fused petals. Kirsten watches for a moment; then, picking up the insect, she crushes it between her thumb and first finger.

Eduardo coughs and shifts his weight. Between the leaves, part of his neck is visible—half a dozen hairs curled in a single spiral.

Kirsten leans forward and touches the back of his neck. Placing the heel of her hand at the base of the spiral, she brushes up his hair, exposing a ring of white flesh at the base of his skull.

The action is completed. Two processes converge at the point of contact.

◆ ◆ ◆

Binary fusion. The blind, unanticipated repetition of patterns that occurs (abruptly, spontaneously) at the intersection of memory and action, as if (by some unexplained process) certain events were preserved as templates. Delayed symmetry. The visceral, kinesthetic persistence of a forgotten motion.

(Colorado, late summer.)

(I am riding slowly up the draw, holding the reins in one hand. The leather strips feel warm, slightly damp. As the horse moves forward, I can feel them press against my fingers, pushing the skin into a series of minute, invisible ridges, shallow depressions that end just behind the second joint.)

(The horse turns and begins to pick its way between the clumps of dry grass and wilted buckbrush. Behind me, I can hear my brother's horse turn to follow. The hooves rasp against the bare rock; there is a rhythmical snapping, the constant steady sound of breaking twigs. Suddenly, the texture and intensity of the noises is altered, muffled slightly. The horses are crossing a layer of pine needles, a dense, slippery mass that absorbs both sound and light, trapping them in a maze of overlapping surfaces. The needles break rapidly with an almost imperceptible click.)

(Lifting my head, I look up along the upper rim of the ridge. The aspen trees have begun to turn. Those at the top have already lost most of their leaves. The branches (bare, slick, tangled together parallactically) spread out to either side like immense white nets, delicate wooden lattices that blow back and forth over the edge of the canyon. Lower down, the trees are still green. Between the two states there appears to be no distinct point of transition, no definite bands of color, no obvious borders. Instead, there is a series of transitional states, a gradient of color and density. The aspen leaves, moving constantly, turning with every shift in the air current, suspended from a single stem) blend together gradually, shifting form dark green to bright yellow, passing through an entire series of intermediate shades.)

(The horses move deliberately, picking their way up between the outcropping rocks. Their hoofs (pointed back at an angle, bent in slightly towards the underside of the body) strike the dry ground with a dull clopping sound, leaving almost no trace on the hardened surface. From time to time (as my brother follows me), I can hear a small twig snap; a few pebbles roll noisily to one side, rattling against the bare rock.)

(The horses move slowly uphill, crossing and recrossing a shallow stream that runs down the center of the draw. Beads of water drip from their hooves and fetlocks. Falling at regular intervals, they form a series of linked semicircles in the dust, long arcs that cut across the stream, interrupted at the apex, continued on either side. As I lean forward (shifting with the moving horse), I feel myself suspended above them, following the same pattern at a different level. The arcs grow smaller, contracting as they dry. I see them clearly, in great detail.)

(Suddenly, a dipper bird appears, skimming just above the surface of the water. It flies rapidly downhill, following the course of the stream, moving up and down erratically, as though catching invisible insects. The horses continue to move forward. Turning abruptly, the bird darts off at an angle. It passes out of focus, a vague, triangular blur.)

(Leaning back, I pull in on the reins, gripping the sides of the horse with my knees and thighs. Moving only the upper portion of my body, I turn to the left, following the flight of the bird, repeating its motion on a reduced scale.)

Prototypic action. The blind, unanticipated initiation of a pattern, kinesthetic correspondence.

(I reach out, spreading my hand flat, fingers extended.)

Template. Intersection.

(My brother pulls up his horse, stopping beside me, motionless, bent slightly forward, his head tilted down towards the saddle horn. He appears to be unaware of the bird, to be concentrating only on the mane of his horse. Still looking to one side, I reach out (palm flat, fingers extended) and place the heel of my hand on the back of his neck, brushing up his hair, exposing the ring of untanned flesh at the base of his skull.)

The two converge. Moving simultaneously, Eduardo and my brother turn towards me.

◆ ◆ ◆

Double exposure.

Moving towards each other, the images intersect, overlap. As Eduardo turns, I see (superimposed on him, slightly displaced) the prismatic diffraction of a remembered body, a persistent afterimage which duplicates (mimetically, arc by arc) each section of his trajectory.

(I lean forward mechanically, pushing aside the bush with both hands.)

Emulsion. The bodies blend together without mixing, sliding across each other like sheets of colored plastic. At the instant of maximum congruence, a kind of focus is established. My brother appears in front of me—a solid, opaque form. Then (suddenly, without transition) there is a slight shift, an almost imperceptible distortion. The frames are transposed, one body substituted for another. Looking up, I see Eduardo leaning over me.

(I touch him methodically, feeling the hair along his wrists and forearms, following the line that radiates out from the center of his body. Eduardo moves closer. His chest is hard, his nipples soft, blunt, inverted. Reaching around him, I can feel the solid, symmetrical curve of his shoulders, the constant (almost peristaltic) motion of his spine.)

Eduardo lifts his head. Still partially screened by the Datura leaves, he looks like a large white insect, a gigantic albino mantis. His eyes are empty, expressionless—highly polished, compound surfaces that reflect only their own internal structure, their own geometric perfection. As he bends over me, I see myself divided into hundreds of identical images, mirrored in infinite regress.

(Eduardo moves closer. Pulling him down on top of me, I open and absorb him.)

♦ ♦ ♦

Getting up from the table, Mark walks to the back of the cabin, bends down, and pulls something out from under one of the cots. Putting it under one arm, he walks quickly towards the door.

(The object is roughly cylindrical. Concealed by the shifting shadows, it appears as a mass of tangled black lines, a coil of fine threads rolled together like a bundle of barbwire. As Mark crosses the room, the light from the lamp enters the roll, projecting moving designs across the floor of the cabin. These patterns (crossed; overlapping; woven into an elastic, expanding mesh) are repeated on the walls and ceiling, breaking the flat surfaces of the room into irregular, disconnected pieces. The light itself seems to be distorted in the process, twisted into cracks and wrinkles, as though somehow it had been crumpled and unfolded. As Mark moves towards the door, it begins to congeal behind him in a flat, uninterrupted block. The fissures contract, leaving an empty, transparent volume, clean, continuous surfaces.

Mark stops. Shifting the mist net, he wedges it firmly between his upper arm and side, pressing the threads into a compact cone. Leaning forward, he walks rapidly out of the cabin.

◆ ◆ ◆

The forest emerges slowly as a series of reflections, optical illusions created at the intersection of air and water. There is a kind of congruence, a systematic blending of forms.

The vine hangs motionless above the surface of the river. Its broad heart-shaped leaves are slightly twisted, the pale green undersides exposed. Near the center of the cable, there is a leaf that seems to belong to another species. Oval, not pointed, it grows straight out as if supported by invisible threads. Seen from below, it appears to be an epiphyte lodged in a notch in the stem, the product of a small, dust-like seed, a minute particle.

(The pods explode serially, following a strict sequence. Floating down from the upper canopy, carried by the wind, the seeds look like motes of dust, a haze of yellow powder that drifts out over the river forming a thin, coherent film. This film (sifting down through the leaves) interrupts the reflections, concealing them behind a floating membrane, a moving skin that washes past the triangle of gravel, that is carried (as a single surface) into the deep pool below the bridge.)

The leaf is torn slightly at one corner, curled in around the edges. Just to the right of center, there are three small brown spots of mold and a long band of black fungus. Nearer the stem, some small aphids have eaten through the leaf coat, exposing the bottom edge of the veins. Two hairs (knobbed at the ends, almost invisible against the background vegetation) stretch out from the base of the leaf, running parallel to the central cable of the main vine.

As the vine swings back and forth in the wind, these hairs appear and disappear, materialize and dissolve, catching the sunlight, reflecting it, moving back into the shadows. They seem to tremble slightly, as though caught in a weak crosscurrent, passing through the pencil-thin strips of light that filter down through the canopy. For a moment, as the vine turns, the hairs shine like pieces of nylon thread. The knobs become more prominent, reflecting surfaces that turn in the air like rods of faceted crystal.

Then the vine swings back into the shadows. The hairs disappear. The wind stops blowing.

Suddenly the leaf flutters. Its movements (isolated, unique) are reflected in the still surface of the river. As if providing a counter motion, a large black fish floats beneath the surface, out of phase, swimming slowly downstream along the bottom without creating a single ripple.

The leaf turns. Lifting itself away from the vine, it exposes six segmented legs. The hairs become antennae, sensitive projections that sweep across the bark, touching it lightly, recording the texture.

Opening its wings, the insect glides out across the water, spinning and falling towards the opposite shore. Although there is no wind, it gives the illusion of being blown to the other side of the river. As the reflection moves across the surface, the insect appears as a falling leaf, a scrap of dead vegetation.

♦ ♦ ♦

Throwing his legs over the edge of the pool, Eduardo slides into the water. Floating at the center of the pond, Kirsten gives no indication that she is aware of his presence. Eyes closed, head back, arms thrust out to either side, she turns slowly clockwise like a radiating spoke.

Eduardo swims just below the surface, moving smoothly without a ripple. Bending at the waist, he dives to the bottom, blending into the shadows of the sunken snags. For a moment there appears to be only one person in the pool—a woman stretched out limply on the surface.

Without warning, Eduardo reappears just behind her head. Reaching out, he places both hands on her shoulders and pushes her body underwater. Kirsten twists over onto her stomach and begins to splash and kick. Both bodies disappear briefly behind a sheet of falling water.

(Upstream the sun has entered the shade of the guayabo trees. The mist net is dry, empty, blowing back and forth in the breeze. Mark pauses on the bridge, holding onto the vine with his left hand. He stands rigidly, taking shallow, incomplete breaths, as if listening to something. The sound of laughter (faint, attenuated, diluted by the wind) is repeated. Mark crosses the river and begins to walk uphill towards the cabin.)

The pool is empty. There are no waves. The surface is perfectly calm except for a slight shift in water level around the edges as if, having been tipped to one side, the pool were regaining its equilibrium. The center appears level, a dense sheet of polished green glass.

Two people are sitting on the opposite shore. Eduardo lies flat on his back, spread out on the rock like a sunning lizard. Kristen bends over him, drying his arms and shoulders with a handful of dry grass. Moving down from the neck, she sops up drops of water from the chest and abdomen, following the line of hair (sparse, blond, almost invisible) that runs down the center of his body like a seam. Pushing against his flesh, she can feel the hard, continuous curve of muscles just below the surface of the skin. As Kirsten touches him, Eduardo relaxes. His muscles blend together beneath her fingers, loose, elastic, moving freely, as though they were no longer attached to a skeleton.

Kirsten lowers her arm. Turning away, she looks out over the surface of the pool. Eduardo remains motionless for a few moments. Then, sitting up, he reaches out over the edge of the rock and picks a handful of grass. Slowly, as though moving with great difficulty, he begins to dry Kirsten's back.

Putting down the water can, Dulce-Maria moves closer to the pool.

The sound of laughter (clear, distinct, undiluted) is repeated.

As if responding to a conditioned reflex, moving automatically, involuntarily, she crouches down behind a large bush. Pushing the leaves apart with one hand, she supports herself against the ground with the other, pushing the tips of her fingers into the cool, damp dirt.

The laughter continues.

Dulce-Maria leans forward slightly, bending her body in a semicircle, moving to one side so that her face is not reflected on the surface of the water.

The girl remains in the same position for some time, looking at something on the opposite bank. Her face (blank, expressionless, immobile) is partially concealed by the overhanging leaves.

Shifting her weight to her heels, Dulce-Maria leans back, and (still bent double) moves backwards slowly, awkwardly, pushing her arms out to either side like a large land crab.

Halfway up the hill, she stands and turns around. The pool is no longer visible; the river is hidden behind a dense band of brush.

As the girl runs upstream towards the bridge, the sun shines across the sides of the water can transforming it into a series of rectangular mirrors, a block of intense light interrupted by spots of rust, distorted at the edges by dents and chips in the metal. Square of light, multiple, symmetrical reflections, are projected onto the tall grasses that grow on either side of the path, thrown against the trunks of trees, across overhanging lianas. Each time the girl takes a step forward, they move horizontally, bobbing up and down, expanding and contracting contrapuntally. From time to time, they disappear completely, absorbed by the shadows of large trees, assimilated, diluted. Then (as if coming from an internal source, generated by a sudden fusion of invisible particles) they reappear, expanding, becoming more intense, hard bright rectangles bordered with a narrow band of blue light that shines with the intensity of a carbon-arc lamp.

◆ ◆ ◆

Small phosphorescent insects are attracted to the headlamp. Moths, flies, and beetles (translucent insects with huge protruding eyes, with cold glowing globes of light that appear erratically, constantly shifting their position, altering their intensity) fly in diminishing circles, moving around the woman's head in layered rings, brushing against her cheeks, breaking their wings against the glass bulb.

Kirsten walks along the edge of the river, moving upstream towards the bridge. In one hand she carries a small three-ring notebook: in the other, an insect net. From time to time, she lifts the net and swings it rapidly around her head, trapping the moths and flies in the mesh. Rolling the insects into a compact ball, Kirsten crushes them in her fist. Then, with a flick of her forearm, she turns the net inside out, shaking the dead insects onto the ground. For a moment the beam is clear; the light shines in a long, uninterrupted band. Suddenly, as if it had entered a cloud of incandescent dust, it is broken by hundreds of minute moving bodies, filled with a new collection of flying insects.

Before Kirsten can lift the net, a large insectivorous bat appears in front of her face. The bat flits back and forth eating some of the larger mosquitoes. Kirsten can see the nose-leaf quivering rhythmically as the bat follows the path of a small fly. The wings extend beyond the edges of the beam, creating the illusion that the animal has been stretched between two parallel poles, hung up to dry like a study skin.

Kirsten turns her head. Flapping its wings, the bat moves back into the darkness, disappearing into the dense shadow of an overhanging Heliconia.

Complete darkness. Ultrasonic pulse. Downward one octave.

The bat flies slowly, scanning the echoes.

Pulse repeated.

As the bat moves forward, the forest (dark, invisible, visually inaccessible) reappears as a series of sonic textures, as an ordered system of resonance and vibration. Color is replaced by pitch; value and saturation become a blending of overtones; distance, depth, and location are determined by binaural differentiation, by a kind of stereophonic separation.

Lowering both its wings simultaneously, the bat swerves sharply. To the left, a tree appears as a band of intense noise, a broad line of maximum reflection that redirects and amplifies the original impulse. The trunk (hard, resistant, dense) produces a sharp, precise echo, a narrow undistorted vibration. The branches are dimmer, more muted, muffled by small patches of silence, the soft absorbent surfaces of vines and leaves. The echoes return more slowly, at a lower frequency. The pattern is wide, diffuse, partially transparent.

Turning suddenly, the bat alters the duration and intensity of the pulses. The sonic grid becomes smaller, more concentrated, reduced to a hemisphere directly in front of the mouth. The rest of the forest becomes a band of indistinct overtones, a single track of undifferentiated background noise.

(The insect appears first as a frequency shift, a progressive change in wavelength. As it passes in front of the bat (moving into the hemisphere of focus) the number of vibrations increases; the pitch is raised; the interval between echoes, shortened.)

The bat doubles the pulse repetition rate. Spreading its fingers, pulling both wing membranes taut, it begins to push itself forward rapidly, without effort.

The pulses overlap.

(Sensitive to the ultrasonic signals of the approaching predator, the moth folds its wings and drops to the forest floor. As it falls, it drifts randomly, generating a confusing pattern of echoes, a dense screen of static.)

Sonic focus. The moving insect is magnified, caught at the exact center of the hemisphere, reproduced in detail as a series of precise, undistorted vibrations.

The bat flies closer, extending one wing. As the moth strikes the membrane, the bat brings its back legs forward, guiding the insect into its mouth. Methodically, with an almost mechanical precision, it bites off the head.

◆ ◆ ◆

Michigan. Late summer.

The beach is covered with ladybugs. They gather in an irregular strip just above the high water mark, massed along the rims of receding waves. The insects cover the mast of the sail boat, clinging to the rigging, concealing the rudder under a sheet of red enamel. As Kirsten bends down, they crawl up the backs of her legs, brushing against her ankles, unfolding soft, pleated wings. The elytra are lifted away from the body, suspended above the expanding membranes like symmetrical shells.

Kirsten turns and looks up the beach. A black line of birds is superimposed on the insects. The line moves forward, absorbing the red mass, leaving a streak of clean white sand along the edge of the water. As she walks towards them, the birds rise simultaneously, wheeling above her head in large, overlapping circles. Each segment of their flight seems to exist in a perpetual present, without cause, without effect, a discontinuous arc arrested at one point in time. It is as if the entire pattern were composed of a series of individual links, connected only by an artificial shift in perspective. Kirsten forces herself to move forward, driving the actions towards a conclusion. The birds hover for a moment, then, turning like a school of fish, they fly out over the water, moving in perfect formation.

Bending down, the boy pulls the mast out from under the hull. Then he turns the boat over, pushing up one edge, lifting it away from his body. Reaching out with both hands, Kirsten guides the falling hull, pushing rigidly against the bottom (wrists straight, fingers extended), controlling the speed and angle of the trajectory. The boat turns slowly, drifts towards the ground as though it were floating through a clear, heavy

81

liquid. It moves in slow motion, expanding out from the center, rotating around an invisible axis.

Shaking the insects off of the rigging, the two children set the sail and shove the boat into the water. It glides forward, creating an almost invisible wake, cutting through a circle of floating ladybugs. Bracing herself against the mast, Kirsten pushes down the center board.

♦ ♦ ♦

Mark is sitting at the table scraping candle wax off the surface with the edge of a rusty dissecting scalpel. He works methodically, running the blade between the boards, working out from his body in a semicircle. Seen from a distance, he seems to be performing a complicated task, an intricate series of motions that require his complete concentration.

Mark tilts the blade, bending his fingers at the second joint. The wax comes up in broken spirals; short, twisted curls frayed along the edges. Some of these curls (following the wake of the moving blade) blow off the table, falling to the floor like shreds of discarded fruit peel.

As Mark works towards the center of the table, his hands (moving closer to the kerosene lamp, growing brighter as they enter the light) appear to be two different sizes. The hand holding the scalpel looks heavy, compact, dense. The other (rotated straight out form the wrist; moving rapidly with a lateral brushing motion) looks partially flattened, as if it had been pressed between heavy weights.

Mark stops and withdraws his hands. To his left (spread out flat on the surface of the table) there is a brown canvas kit containing two pairs of scissors (large and small), a spool of black cotton thread, a pair of forceps, three clamps, and a paper packet of needles (assorted sizes). Near the bottom of the kit, there is a rectangle on which is printed the information: "Mycrosyn: Surgical Blades. 6 Blades Size 11." Inside, wrapped in heavy waxed paper, there are three new blades and two used ones.

Directly in front of Mark (just inside the circle of light) there is a partially stuffed bird skin. The head has been filled with cotton (a compact white lump, conforming to the contours of the skull, hidden behind a layer of green feathers). Beside the bird, there is a broken needle, a roll of blue tissue paper, an empty aguardiente bottle, half a box of matches, an unglazed bowl of cornmeal, and a pack of blank labels.

Mark coughs and shifts his weight, tipping his chair forward on two legs. Balancing his body above the surface of the table, he rocks back and forth slightly, as if suspended from an invisible string. A string of finished bird skins (hanging just above his head, tied together by a piece of nylon fish line) moves in counter rhythm, duplicating his gesture in a continuous series of mirror images.

Mark is alone in the cabin.

From time to time, he turns his head as if looking for something on the porch. Finally, he gets up from the table and walks to the back of the room. His footsteps sound hollow, disproportionately loud. Mark stops. The only noise in the cabin is the buzzing of the lamp, the dampened hum of nocturnal insects.

♦ ♦ ♦

As Mark stops, his presence is extended, propagated as a series of sine waves, minute variations in temperature and pressure that expand spherically through space, penetrating the walls of the cabin, moving out into the forest.

Macaws, toucans, motmots, snakes, salamanders, frogs, spiders, lacewings, pseudoscorpions, seed ticks, tipulids, ants, moths, termites, rhinoceros beetles, bats, caimans, lizards, pacas, and peccaries become conscious of a faint, repetitive perturbation, a periodic influence. Each form of life receives the sensation differently (as a pulsation of invisible red light, as an intense ultrasonic vibration) and each responds according to its own internal structure.

Even static, sessile organisms—the grasses, lilies, and palms growing along the bank of the river, the parallel-veined Heliconia, the red bract wild ginger, lianas, epiphytes, acacia trees, kapok, catalpa, cecropia, jacquinia—even the huge madron trees at the center of the forest react to a certain spectrum of his presence, make silent, infinitesimal adjustments.

The waves continue to spread, radiating out uniformly in all directions. Mark stands at the center, motionless, nucleic.

♦ ♦ ♦

The boat moves rapidly away from the shore. Kirsten leans back against the mast and watches the cottages shrink. Collapsing in on one another, they merge into a continuous strip, a narrow, multicolored band that blends into the background vegetation.

Suddenly a man in a blue sweatshirt runs down to the edge of the water. Cupping his hands to his mouth, he yells something in the direction of the boat. The sound is distorted by the wind, reduced to a faint squeak, an incoherent band of white noise. Kirsten bends forward. From a distance, the man looks like a small, agitated insect, a puppet jerked by invisible strings. His motions seems to be the products of an occult variation of the alphabet of the deaf, silent, incomprehensible, hermetic. Leaning out over the water, the man repeats his question. This time no sound reaches the boat.

The waves grow larger. Between the billows, the shoreline disappears completely. Letting go of the rudder, the boy yells something in a loud voice. Kirsten lifts her head. His words are drowned out by water crashing over the prow. A huge wave suddenly appears, rising up above the mast in a solid wall, a thick barrier of green glass that curves out infinitely in all directions. The boat stops, frozen at the bottom of the wave.

♦ ♦ ♦

Walking to the far end of the kitchen, Kirsten opens the wooden shutters. She works in complete darkness, pushing her fingers into the knot, pulling apart the leather thongs with her knuckles. The entire process takes place invisibly, guided by tactile perceptions. When the strings are disentangled, Kirsten leans forward and pushes against the wall. A crack of light appears directly in front of her, parallel to her body. Kirsten continues to push with the ball of her hand. The crack widens, expands into a rectangle. Kirsten leans out the window and ties back the shutters on either side. Then, reaching up along the inside of the wall, she draws a piece of netting over the opening.

As the light enters the room, various objects appear, moving out of the darkness. On the counter in front of the window there is a galvanized basin, a dipper (handle missing), two tin cups, a scrap of dirty sacking, a bar of soap (smooth, gray cube, chipped at the corners), an empty bottle, and a bucket of water. The top of the bucket is covered with a square of green nylon screen, weighted down at the center with an empty coffee can.

A shelf runs along the right hand side of the room just above shoulder level. Moving from the door to the window, there is a pile of unwashed potatoes, a cloth bag full of black beans, a tin of rice, two onions, half a bottle of oil, a small basin, several cans, three chocolate bars, a bottle of aguardiente, two plates, a broken candle, some packets of dried soup, a small bag of coffee, and a box of matches. Hanging above the shelf (suspended from a rusty nail) there is a stalk of green bananas, two ripe coconuts, and a string of dried peppers.

Turning her back to the window, Kirsten reaches out and picks up a box of matches. As she turns, her body contracts, shrinking to a solid gray line. A metal bar seems to have been placed across the far end of the window. As the turn is completed, the body expands, filling the entire rectangle with a flat, featureless surface.

Kirsten walks to the opposite side of the kitchen and lights both burners of the portable stove. The gas ignites with a sucking sound, a band of bright blue light that seems to move out from the head of the match in two symmetrical arcs, merging into a perfect circle. The face of the woman suddenly appears, perfectly distinct, suspended over the surface of the table.

To the left of the stove there is a bowl full of black beans and water. The beans press against the side of the bowl in a compact, swollen mass, forming half a sphere, a semisolid volume of discrete particles. Moving rapidly, as if her actions had been reduced to a set of efficient reflexes, Kirsten pushes the beans to one side and picks up the coffee pot. Her arm interrupts the light from the burners, crossing in front of the flame, casting indistinct shadows (moving lines of blue and gray; solid, overlapping bands that conform to the contours of the room, sliding over the walls and ceiling of the kitchen). The movement is multiplied, expanded in all directions, projected onto the bright surfaces of tin cups (curved, convex, following the bend of the rim, distorted out at an angle), spread across bags and cans, broken into fragments by the window. As the flames move, the shadows flicker, duplicating every change in the angle and intensity of the light.

Bending over the stove, Kirsten places the coffee pot on the burner.

◆ ◆ ◆

The wave breaks over the prow of the boat. Kirsten is caught in a block of boiling white water, thrown back against the mast as though her body were a flimsy colorless strip, weightless, invisible. The water expands, filling an indefinite period of time, congealing around the boat like a layer of lucite. All motion stops; sequence is suspended. The process continues as a series of snapshots arranged in chronological order.

Resting at the center of the crest, Kirsten is no longer conscious of her body, no longer able to separate it from the static liquid. Her kinesthetic sense is anesthetized, her arms and legs dissolved in a motionless solution, a uniform mass without discrete parts. Suddenly the equilibrium is ruptured. The boat passes through the wave, moving out of the water into the air.

Kirsten opens her eyes. Almost immediately her brother reappears, crouched in the stern, his arms and legs wrapped around the rudder. To his left the bailing can is bobbing up and down on the surface of the water, following in the wake of the boat. Kirsten smiles and leans forward. Letting go of the rudder, her brother begins to crawl towards the bow. The boat rocks from side to side. Suspended between two waves, it appears to be floating calmly on the flat surface of a small pond.

◆ ◆ ◆

Something white is moving below the surface of the forest pool. Eduardo leans forward, following the indistinct shape as it floats over the dark lines of submerged logs. The body seems to be buoyed up on a grid of shadows, suspended above the bottom of the pool by a huge net. The mesh is irregular, a heap of jack straws, strips of bone and black ivory woven together haphazardly, extending out in all directions along a multidimensional warp. The moving body (floating away from the surface, reduced to a solid white line) glides between the interstices like an erratic shuttle.

As Kirsten forces her way down to the bottom, her hair trails out behind her, rising above her head like a mass of floating weeds. Arching her back, she increases the angle of her descent, pushing her arms out to either side in wide, even circles. The hands are back to back, cupped slightly, thumbs down, fingers curved in towards the wrists. As Kirsten swims her hair moves from side to side, following the underwater wake, drifting away from her skull like a bundle of inverted nematophores.

Reaching the bottom, Kirsten stops. Drawing her arms in to her sides, she hangs just above the submerged rocks, a perpendicular line that begins to float slowly towards the surface. Kirsten rolls over on her back. Her body seems to change color, to fade into a dull white band. Her breasts blend into her chest, pale, loose, swollen out like the underbelly of a filefish.

As Kirsten floats towards the surface, her features are reduced to six black circles, darks spots distributed unevenly over a flattened surface. These circles appear to expand slowly, to spread out from the eyes, mouth, underarms, and crotch as the body rises. Still submerged, Kirsten turns slightly, pushing her arms out to either side, as if (no longer moving) she could arrest the expansion of her features with a gesture.

Eduardo bends over the water. Looking up, Kirsten can only see a vague shadow, a reticulated shape that seems to momentarily break the tension of the surface.

◆ ◆ ◆

A mist net is strung along the opposite side of the river. Hundreds of fine black threads (invisible against the background vegetation) are suspended between the guayabo trees. Intersecting at right angles, two sets of parallel lines cross to form a huge rectangle, bloated into three dimensions at the center, stretched out along the edges.

The net hangs like an immense spider web, tenuous, complex, deceptively fragile. As it moves (swaying back and forth, blowing out across the water) it casts thin, rod-shaped shadows, multiple transects that fall across a transparent block of empty space, dividing the area into a series of regular cubes. The center appears and disappears, fading into the lianas and epiphytes, condensing into broken threads that run across the leaves like minute cracks, crazing the glazed surface. Only the edges (pulled taut, woven back on themselves) are clear, steady, persistent.

Suddenly a hummingbird appears, flying straight towards the upper right-hand corner of the net. As it strikes the webbing, its flight continues for a moment without interruption. The bird moves forward rapidly as if unaware of the surrounding threads. Then, abruptly, the net closes in around the moving body, stopping it, pushing it backwards. From a distance, the bird appears to collide with an imaginary obstacle, to rebound from an invisible surface. Struggling violently, it becomes inextricably snarled. The wings are pinned to the side of the body, the legs bent slightly, pushed forward against the breast. The head protrudes through the mesh, moving convulsively.

Blending into the blue and green feathers, the threads disappear, creating the illusion that the bird is hanging without support, hovering several feet above the forest floor. As the animal twists its body, lower its head, the net becomes more tightly knotted around the neck and bill. This final effort (paroxysmal, spasmodic) causes a kind of involuntary rotation. The bird turns completely upside down, folding the threads double, pulling the mesh into a tight ring of triangles. Motion stops. All points converge on the concealed body.

(Near the upper right-hand corner of the net, there is a clump of tangled threads. From time to time, something blue appears between the interstices—a bit of feather that catches and refracts the light like the tip of a prism. The rest of the web is empty. Along the opposite edge, there is a long tear, a lateral row of broken threads that runs from the top corner to the center.

Although (standing on the bridge, looking out towards the far bank of the river) the net itself is invisible, the break in the mesh is obvious. A strip of the forest seems to have been brought into focus, magnified in a narrow band of unobstructed light. Within the confines of this band, the outlines are more distinct, differences in color and texture more prominent. A large banana leaf (partly traversed by the tear) appears to be streaked with clear enamel. As the net blows out across the water, the glaze moves slowly over the leaf, an immense larva that crosses the surface without conforming to it.)

Under the net, partially concealed in the grass, there is a piece of rotting fruit. The outer rim is covered with fire ants. Near the center there are several small flies, a wasp, and a large brown beetle. The fruit seems to have been divided into invisible sub-territories. Seen from above, the arrangement of the insects appears to be regular, recurrent, almost systematic.

The bird struggles once again, shaking the net.

♦ ♦ ♦

Kirsten picks up an orange. Bending forward (moving only the upper portion of her body, her head, neck, and shoulders) she breaks the tough outer skin with her front teeth and begins to peel it back, exposing the individual sections one by one. The ten units (each crescent-shaped, each swollen slightly at the center) are encased in a tough white membrane, a cohesive sheath that binds them into a single sphere. Beneath this primary covering, there is a second layer of closely interwoven threads, a continuous venation that appears as a net of small white fibers, opaque strips that cross and recross, moving randomly over the surface of the fruit. Between the interstices, the inner pulp curves out, dense, compressed, resilient.

Kirsten works steadily, stripping off the thick covering, working her way towards the bottom of the sphere. Balanced in her hand, turned away from her body, the unpeeled portion of the fruit feels like a piece of warm rubber—malleable, waxy, dull; it presses against her skin, conforming to the contours of her palm, following the semicircular curve of her fingers, assimilating them in a single texture.

Kirsten rotates the fruit slightly, shifting it to one side. Each section (partially revealed, expanding out from the center, inflated, protruding, pointed at both ends) appears as a convex surface. As Kirsten squeezes the fruit, these crescents contract, grow more compact, less detached. The membrane (strained by the pressure) ruptures in several places revealing the moist inner surface of the pulp.

Kirsten puts down the orange. Picking up a scrap of discarded skin, she crumples it between her thumb and index finger, twisting it slightly, releasing a spurt of oil into the air, a fine volatile spray that covers her hands and forearms with the scent of oranges. Slowly, as though performing a complex operation, she begins to detach the individual sections, stripping back the membrane with the tip of one nail, picking off the stringy placenta. She works with intense concentration, repeating the same motions, automatically, without hesitation, as though confining her actions to certain pre-established patterns. Each time the bend of the fingers, the angle of the arm, the inclination of the body is the same. Each time her work is thorough, precise, without variation or deviation.

The segments are detached one by one (petals pulled off calyx, falling away from the center; the perturbation of a static symmetry; irreversible, descending arcs), placed carefully on the blue and white kerchief. Kirsten pulls the corners of the cloth straight, forming a perfect square. Bending closer, she begins to count the segments, arranging them in two equal rows. The sphere now exists only in two dimensions, a series of disjointed fragments spread out over a single surface.

(Released from the skin, the drops of oil continue to float, drifting out over the surface of the pool. Instead of falling, they are caught up in imperceptible crosscurrents, blown in all directions, spreading and turning in the sunlight like an expanding nebula, a whorl of colorless scent. Kirsten bends forward, sitting at the center of the spiral, frozen for a moment, a static point at the center of the vortex. Her necks and breasts (bare, shining, covered with irregular splotches of light) are coated with an even film, glazed and preserved under a thin layer of oil.)

Suddenly, without transition, movement is reintroduced.

Turning around, Kirsten leans over and dips her hands into the pool. She lifts them out, shakes off the excess water, and begins to dry her fingers methodically on the edge of the kerchief. Pointing in the direction of the fruit, she says something to Eduardo.

(Dulce-Maria shifts her weight to her heels, leans back and (still facing the pool) begins to crawl slowly backwards through the dense brush. Halfway up the hill, she stands up and turns around; Eduardo and Kirsten are no longer visible; the river is hidden behind a band of overhanging trees.)

◆ ◆ ◆

(Dulce-Maria, Eduardo's sister, who came to me unobserved, ignored, unrecognized; in whom I failed to perceive the invisible mechanism of focus; who became (obliquely, unconsciously) the organizing principle, the primary matrix.)

The girl walks up the hill, following the path to the cabin. As she moves, the tall grasses on either side bend over the edge of the trail, concealing the lower portion of her body. Only her head (small, dark, a black flower with a bale brown center), her neck (thin, narrow, translucent), and part of her dress (a scrap of unbleached cotton) are suspended above the surface.

As she walks, Dulce-Maria appears to be swimming through bands of floating kelp, through islands of fucus and sea lettuce. Wrist bent, palm stretched out flat, fingers joined, she cuts a channel through the grasses, pushing them to one side, moving into the open space. Her hands and arms (blurred by their own motion) seem to diffuse through the blades, to pass (divided into thousands of tiny strips) through a series of filters, dissolved, fragmented.

Dulce-Maria touches the blades. They bend slightly, then close together behind her. A white dot (the bright, reduced reflection of the sun) moves over the curved surfaces, passing from base to tip. From a distance, the body moving through the clearing (the small, indistinct body of the moving child) seems to be surrounded by a fringe of expanding light, a luminous swarm of small white insects.

As she draws closer to the cabin, Dulce-Maria appears to grow larger, to be magnified, extended beyond her original dimensions. Her face becomes more distinct; the eyes appear; lashes are formed along the rims of the lids; mouth, nose, and cheeks emerge; the

97

bone structure (fine, curved, narrow bones) becomes obvious.

(On her upper lip, a small birthmark runs to the base of her left nostril. From a distance, it is almost invisible, a partial curve, a blurred white line, a single strip of light (ophidian, incomplete) moving across her face.)

Dulce-Maria reaches the steps of the cabin and stops. Putting down her sisal bag, she steps onto the porch.

◆ ◆ ◆

(Dulce-Maria. Who saw everything; in whose eyes I failed to recognize my own reflection.)

She steps onto the porch.

A face appears behind the screen. As it moves, the nylon mesh breaks the image up into a network of wavy lines, into overlapping moiré patterns. Distorted slightly, diffracted, the face appears to be floating just below the surface of a shallow pool.

Dulce-Maria lifts her head and looks into the cabin. The light (which radiates from the interior) is absorbed by her eyes as energy, transmitted, reproduced in her mind as a coherent image. Categories are invoked in her cerebral cortex; spatial relationships established; a context (of patterns and positions) is generated. The face appears distinctly, perceived as a separate object, a cohesive, self-contained form. Almost simultaneously (as if it were a surrounding aura) depth appears; perspective is introduced; continuity through time (absent from the primary reflections of the surface of the eyes) is created by memory.

Mark opens the door. Dulce-Maria perceives him as a blank white form, an undifferentiated shape moving across a black background.

Automatically, instinctively, her pupils dilate. As the amount of light projected onto the retina is increased, a more detailed image is produced.

Dulce-Maria lifts her head and looks at Mark. Her brain bends the light, structures it, imposes continuities, generates (as does the convex surface of her cornea) unanticipated curves, shifting proportions.

♦ ♦ ♦

Mark is sitting at the table drinking aguardiente. On the floor, slightly to one side, there is a canteen, a pair of dirty wool socks, and a rusty machete. As Mark leans back (shifting his weight, throwing his body away from the table), the leg of his chair presses against the tip of the blade, lifting the handle away from the floor. The machete quivers, describing a series of rapid, incomplete arcs, as though coming to rest at the center of a target.

Picking up a can of sardines, Mark begins to remove the lid, twisting the soft tin around the handle of the key in an uneven spiral. The edges (pushed together in a flattened cone) extend out over the edge like the threads of a screw. Holding the can flat against the surface of the table, Mark pushes out at a right angle. His movements are jerky, discontinuous, as if he were applying too much pressure, bending the lid unnecessarily. Suddenly he stops, poised over the can, his wrists held rigidly at right angles. He seems to be lost in the middle of an action he cannot remember initiating.

The lid folds back exposing half the fish. Picking up a sardine between his thumb and first finger, he drops it into his mouth, washing it down with a swig of aguardiente. As he lifts the bottle, a small line of bubbles slides along the side, following the curve of the glass, merging into a flattened oval at the bottom. Seen from above (looking down through the liquid), the face appears as a blank pink circle, a mass of flesh without individual features.

Pressing his body against the back of the chair, he takes shallow, incomplete breaths, as if listening for something. Then, without warning, Mark gets up and walks to the door. A small girl in an unbleached cotton smock is standing on the porch looking into the cabin.

100

Her face (seen through the green nylon screen) is broken into a network of wavy lines, into moiré patterns that move across her cheeks and lips like bands of reflected light. Seen from the inside of the cabin, she appears to be hiding behind a net of geometrically arranged vines.

Mark opens the door. As Dulce-Maria enters the cabin, her eyes dilate, accommodating to the darkness of the interior. The pupils float out over the iris, expanding from the center. The girl walks across the threshold. Her bare feet make slight sucking noises on the cool floor.

Mark says something in Spanish, pointing in the direction of the river. Turning suddenly, Dulce-Maria walks out of the cabin. Holding onto the doorframe with both hands, he repeats his question. Without looking back, the girl bends down and picks up her sisal bag. Running down the steps, she disappears into the tall grass.

Mark sits down on the porch and begins to drink. On the step beside him there is a can of sardines, a canvas bag, and two dead birds.

◆ ◆ ◆

Below the cabin, on the opposite side of the river, the birds move through the forest.

(Scarlet tanagers, saltatores, yellow-crowned euphonias, warblers, caiques, grassquits, tinamous, vultures, zapoyolitos, kites, hawks, laughing falcons, caracaras, guans, doves, macaws, parrots, swifts, smooth-billed anis, barbthroats, jacobins, trogons, motmots, sicklebills, jacamars, aracaris, toucans, golden-napped woodpeckers, honeycreepers, antshrikes, hummingbirds, manakins, flycatchers, swallows, greenlets, cazadoras—the canopy is split, divided into an infinite number of planes. Confined to different levels (intersecting, partially coincident) the animals are superimposed on one another, stratified according to species.)

The birds fly between the trees, perceiving them in terms of density rather than color, watching the vegetation blend into a series of overlapping bands, merge into two dense webs of leaves and brush bound together by an ascending reticulum of trunks and lianas. At the edges, the secondary growth forms a kind of border, an irregular margin that runs along the rim of the river. Emerging section by section, the forest appears as a net, an immense, three-dimensional grid.

As the birds move forward, morphology is replaced by density, by pointillistic distribution. Objects cease to exist; individual forms are incorporated into larger patterns, synthetically arranged. Depth, in turn, becomes a function of darkness, a correlate of opacity. Isolated plants are colorless, empty, insubstantial.

(Kirsten steps onto the bridge. She appears as a single stem, rigid, leafless, almost invisible.)

♦ ♦ ♦

Screaming harshly, a pair of small green parrots crosses the river. As the birds enter the guayabo trees along the opposite bank, their call notes are softened, muffled, absorbed by lianas, the multiple, overlapping surfaces of twigs and leaves.

Kirsten stops in the middle of the bridge, holding onto the handrail, balanced at the exact center.

(The rail is a piece of vine stretched between two wooden posts. Hanging out over the water, it forms an arc across the river, a moving parabola, distorted by the current, reflected from the surface as a series of broken lines, partial, incomplete segments. From time to time, the lines merge, joining to complete the curve. Then, as the wind shifts, they separate again, break into fragments, dissolve.)

(The vine moves, swinging out over the water, rotating so that the underside is partially exposed. Along the bottom, a line of wet clay protrudes slightly, running along the bark lengthwise like an unfinished seam.)

The handrail moves back over the floor of the bridge, gaining momentum, drifting to one side. Before the motion can be completed, Kirsten stops it. As she grabs the rail (pulling it toward her, extending the original arc), her fingers break through the mud tube, penetrating the dark, moist interior of the termite trail. Soft white workers begin to spill out randomly across the undersurface of the vine, blindly nudging and smelling, moving out of the broken tube in a continuous stream. Almost immediately, as if responding to some sort of signal, the soldiers appear, spewing out of either end of the broken tunnel, climbing over the workers and pushing them to one side.

Kirsten bends down and carefully picks up a soldier between her thumb and index finger. She holds it for a moment in the palm of her hand, then flicks it over the side of the bridge into the river.

(Each leg of the falling insect casts a thin, hair-like shadow. These same shadows are repeated, multiplied over the surface of the vine. They stretch out across the smooth bark, expanding as the workers spread in all directions, a tangled net of moving lines that bind the broken ends of the tube together.)

Bending over again, Kirsten picks up another soldier. She places the insect on the palm of her left hand and begins to examine it with a small hand lens.

(The features are curved, distorted, each detail magnified. A nose-like projection appears to extend from the front of the head; the mandibles are large, elongated.)

Kirsten turns her hand slightly, shaking the insect back into the hollow. Leaning forward, she moves the lens closer.

(Light is reflected from the smooth portions of the exoskeleton, refracted into prismatic bands which appear to bend, conforming to the edge of each separate segment. The termite appears to be artificial, a glass insect coated with a thin film of colored lacquer, glazed with a hard, semi-transparent resin.)

Folding back her thumb, Kirsten flicks the insect over the side of the bridge into the river.

♦ ♦ ♦

(The forest continues to congeal without any specific sexuality, androgynous, sustained by internal conjugation, by the simultaneous union of all parts. It develops systematically, embryonically, without artifice, maintained by a genderless, gametic continuity.)

I stop in the middle of the bridge.

On the opposite side of the river, Eduardo appears, running along the bank, moving downstream towards the pool. As he passes between the trees, the forest surrounds him, cutting his body into fragments, blotting it out with leaves, lianas, huge white trunks wedged into gigantic prop roots. He appears as a series of disconnected lines, partial, incomplete. Only parts of his body are visible—a hand, a scrap of bare chest, an ear, a knee, a piece of one arm.

Emerging from the brush, Eduardo enters a small clearing. Suddenly, with no sense of transition, he is reassembled, reorganized into a complete, coherent object. As he moves away from me, crossing the open space, he seems to condense in a cylinder of illuminated dust, to precipitate inside a narrow glass tube.

(The light enters the clearing through a hole in the upper canopy, sliding down along the leaves and branches, falling directly, constantly, a perfectly perpendicular stream. As Eduardo passes under it, it covers him with a thin, opaque membrane, a flexible exoskeleton. Slipping down his bare back, moving across his haunches, the light runs over his legs, filling in the shadows, coating his ankles with an oily film. Every hair stands out separately, ciliate, magnified. Together they form a fine, bright fringe, a corona that extends and distorts the contours of his body.)

As he passes through the clearing, Eduardo seems to enter a different temporal sequence, to move in slow motion. His body stops, arrested indefinitely in one position, confined to a single posture. Closing in from all directions, the surrounding space becomes viscous, amberoid, preservative.

(Eduardo leans forward, hands thrown out to either side, head back, mouth open. Stopped in the process of falling, he appears to be suspended from invisible strings, an Olympic diver caught in midair by a high-speed camera. Eduardo moves down an infinite incline, across a perpetually expanding distance.)

Reaching the edge of the clearing (reaching it without appearing to travel towards it), he blends back into the shadows. For a moment he is only party assimilated by the forest, held in a kind of organic equilibrium. Then, as if repeating the original pattern, his body breaks into segments, dissolves, and disappears.

♦ ♦ ♦

Bending over the stove, Kirsten places the coffee pot on the burner. Then, pulling the corncob stopper out of an old aguardiente bottle, she pours some vegetable oil into the skillet. The oil spreads rapidly, covering the black cast iron bottom with a shallow, viscous glaze.

(Kirsten moves rapidly, with an almost mechanical precision, as if her actions had been reduced to a set of efficient reflexes. Each motion (the lifting of the arm, the pouring of the oil, the tilting of the skillet) seems to initiate the next, to form part of a chain of kinesthetically encoded patterns, a mutually dependent sequence of conditioned responses. It is as if, having once initiated her deeds, Kirsten no longer stands outside them, no longer evaluates, directs, or controls. Instead (freed from the usual necessity of conscious regulation), she appears to merge with her own movements, to be absorbed in them, directed by them, to become (at least temporarily) the simultaneous locus of object and action.

Leaning forward over the tabletop, Kirsten cuts a green cooking banana into two inch pieces. Dusting each piece with flour, she crushes it flat with the ball of her hand and puts it into the oil to fry. Walking to the opposite side of the kitchen, she reaches into the basin (pushing aside the layer of large green leaves, the smooth, cool surfaces of concealed eggs) and (feeling blindly, guided by tactile sensations) lifts out a block of white goat cheese. The cheese feels heavy, dense, elastic, the surface resilient, difficult to penetrate. As Kirsten turns back towards the stove, she appears to be holding a lump of raw rubber.

Frying a piece of the cheese, Kirsten places it on the plate beside the bananas. Then, pouring herself a cup of boiling coffee, she turns off the burners and walks out of the kitchen. As she passes the door of the cabin, she can see Mark (his features blurred and distorted by the green nylon screen, filtered through a fine, colored mesh) sitting on the porch, propped up against a post. From this angle the empty aguardiente bottle and the tin of sardines are not visible.

Moving to the back of the cabin, Kirsten sits down on her cot, balancing the tin plate between her knees. She begins to eat slowly, picking up the greasy food with her fingers, one piece at a time. The cabin is very hot and still. The air seems to have been compressed between the walls, condensed into a heavy, clear liquid. As the sun outside begins to set, the light in the cabin becomes less intense. Shadows grow longer, merging into a solid plane of darkness. Suddenly, as if responding to a cue, the noises begin: the shrill whine of nocturnal insects; the clinking of frogs; the triadic call-note of a distant tinamou. The noises move up from the river, out from the edge of the forest, covering the cabin with an invisible sheath of sound.

Kirsten continues to eat, picking up the greasy food one piece at a time.

♦ ♦ ♦

Mark crosses the river and begins to check the nets. He moves slowly along the bank, as though maintaining his balance with great difficulty, putting one foot directly in front of the other, creating an imaginary ledge.

Working methodically, he scans every inch of the mesh. (The net blows out towards him, covering his face with fine, invisible threads, with strands of spider web that stick to the forehead and cheeks. Mark continues to walk at a steady rate, parallel to the river, indifferent, impervious, moving through the forest as though propelled through a perfect vacuum, frictionless, uniform, inertial. The net blows back into the shadows of the overhanging trees, disappearing, blending into the background vegetation.)

Reaching out (arms lifted out from the shoulders at an obtuse angle, elbows locked), Mark removes a small blue and green hummingbird from the upper right-hand corner of the net. He cuts around the body with the tip of his machete, breaking the strands in an even, regular circle. The bird struggles, pushing the tips of its wings through the mesh, turning at the center like an eccentric axle, a bent, erratic spindle.

(Standing on the bridge, looking out over the water, the circular break in the mesh is clearly visible. A piece of the forest seems to have been brought into focus, magnified in a clear sphere of unobstructed light. The leaves look brighter, more distinct; they bend slightly, conforming to an invisible curve, caught in a moving globe of transparent glass. As the net blows in and out of the shadows, the globe rotates, expanding and contracting, passing through the ordered gradations of perspective. The center is static, flat, a set point surrounded by a succession of variable rims. The break moves across the leaves, cutting them into a series of concentric sections.)

Holding the bird tightly, Mark smothers it in his hand. Then, with his thumb and index finger, he begins to disentangle the body from a cocoon of tangled threads. The bird emerges bit by bit—a mass of blue and green feathers, gray breast, iridescent gorget, the red, conical bill. Balancing the specimen on his knees, Mark unfolds his pocket knife and slits open the nostrils. Working rapidly, he picks up several small white particles with the tip of a camel's hair brush and drops them into a plastic bottle full of alcohol. Then, screwing down the top with a sharp, clockwise twist, he holds the container up to the light and inspects the contents.

(On the opposite side of the river, Dulce-Maria appears suddenly, walking slowly through the underbrush.)

Moving along the edge of the bank, Mark unsnaps the flap of his canvas gas-mask bag and drops in the hummingbird headfirst. As they enter the shadows, the feathers lose their fluorescence, fading to a uniform gray. Merging with the sides and bottom of the bag, they appear to adopt a sort of protective coloration, to blend into the background, opening concealed chromatophores.

Mark begins to cross the bridge. Reaching the middle, he stops, holding tightly onto the vine with his left hand. He stands rigidly, taking shallow, incomplete breaths as if listening to something. The sound of laughter (faint, attenuated, diluted by the wind) is repeated. Crossing the river, Mark walks uphill towards the cabin.

(Upstream, above the bridge, the sun (sinking below the horizon) enters the shadows of the overhanging guayabo trees. The mist net is empty. Dried by the descending sun, the threads move freely, blowing out over the water.)

◆ ◆ ◆

The net bag is tied to the end of the stick with two strips of peeled bark. As Dulce-Maria crosses the bridge, it swings out over the surface of the river, moving in a long, steady arc, oscillating like a pendulum. From a distance, the girl appears to be carrying a large tanager nest, an oval mass of closely meshed fibers.

Balancing herself, holding tightly onto the vine rail, Dulce-Maria walks slowly, stepping methodically, one foot in front of the other. She seems to pick her route with intense concentration, with an almost mechanical precision.

Reaching the far end of the bridge, Dulce-Maria stops and lifts her head. The movement, reflected in her eyes as a series of shifting images, is doubled and reduced, constricted to the limits of the pupil. As she enters the shade of the overhanging trees, the reflection expands, dilating until it fills the entire iris. The sisal bag (distorted slightly by the convex nature of the cornea) is reduced to a white line, a solid strip projected onto a clear, curved surface.

Dulce-Maria walks at a constant rate, holding the stick away from her body, locking her elbows rigidly.

Suddenly the regular swinging motion is interrupted. the bag contracts convulsively, bending at the middle, setting up a whole series of disruptive counter-rhythms.

Wedging the end of the stick between two prop roots, Dulce-Maria moves closer to the edge of the pool, silently pushing aside the underbrush with the flat of her hand.

The sound of laughter is repeated, amplified.

To the left, partially concealed behind a screen of lianas, the bag continues to move erratically, twisting back and forth as if something inside were trying to get out.

♦ ♦ ♦

Motioning towards the fruit, Kirsten says something to Eduardo. Her hands and arms do not move; they remain folded over her stomach, wrists bent, fingers curved tightly around her elbows. Kirsten shifts her weight, pointing with her entire body.

As Eduardo reaches out to pick up a segment of the orange, she looks away from him, turning in a semicircle. Lifting her hand to her mouth, she spits several small seeds into the cupped palm. The seeds (pale, white, oval) are divided into sections, regular parallel ridges that meet in a point at one end. Covered with clear, sticky syrup, they cling to the surface of the skin, moving slightly as the hand opens and closes.

Picking up the seeds one at a time, Kirsten wets them with the tip of her tongue, sucking off the sugary coating. Then, contracting her lips, she spits them into the pool, pushing her whole body forward, leaning out over the water. As it falls, each seed forms a ring of circles, a series of expanding disks that move out from a common center, passing over her reflection, distorting it in all directions. The face seems to hover above the surface, stretched, extended, magnified. As the ripples impinge on it, the jaw dissolves; the cheeks are flattened; the hair (caught at the outer rim) is corrugated, bent into regular, equally curved ridges and hollows. The features are blurred; the head reduced to a black point on a plane surface.

Kristen leans back; the point disappears completely.

Reaching into the grass, Eduardo picks up a large green fruit. He lifts it slowly, pulling against an invisible force, pushing it up out of the shadows. Placing the fruit on the surface of the rock, he reaches out again.

(The fruit rolls to one side exposing a small round scar at the bottom, a shallow depression that marks the point where it has been attached to a stem. Near the upper end of the depression there is a brown spot, a bit of discolored, bruised skin. The rest of the fruit is smooth, waxy, unblemished.)

Picking up his machete, Eduardo splits it in half with one blow. Juice spurts in all directions, covering the edge of the blade, the end of the handle, the top and sides of the rock. The fruit falls into two equal hemispheres revealing a bright red pulp, a moist, grainy center surrounded by a pale green band of peel.

Picking up one of the halves, Eduardo offers it to Kirsten.

◆ ◆ ◆

Mark reaches out and picks up the bottle of aguardiente.

Pulling out the stopper with his front teeth, he tilts back his head and pours some of the clear liquid down his throat. Then, still holding onto the dirty glass neck, he reaches up with his opposite arm and wipes off his mouth with the back of his hand, pulling his shirt cuff across his lips, stretching them into an artificial grimace, a rubber smile.

On the steps beside him, balanced against the edge of the porch, there is half a can of sardines, a brown canvas bag, and two dead birds. Picking up a sardine between his thumb and first finger, Mark drops it headfirst into his mouth, washing down the fish with another swing of aguardiente. Then placing the bottle carefully on the ground, he reaches into his pocket and takes out a cigarette. His motions have a kind of drunken precision, a mechanical, mnemonic regularity. Reaching out again towards the sardines, he displays the caution of an acrobat looking for a handhold.

As he fumbles in the oil, Mark cuts the knuckle of his index finger on the jagged edge of the lid. Without changing his posture, without any indication that he is aware of the accident, he continues to grope for a sardine. Tilting the can, he pours the liquid onto the ground and shakes the remaining fish forward, out from under the cover.

Kirsten appears, walking towards the cabin. Her wet hair is tied back from her face with a blue and white kerchief. In one hand, she carries an aluminum insect net; in the other a small plastic notebook.

Mark looks up from the sardines. He says something in a low voice. Without answering, Kirsten bends down and picks up the bottle of aguardiente. Lifting the greasy rim to her lips, she takes a large gulp.

Mark repeats his question. Kirsten puts down the bottle abruptly and walks into the cabin. Leaning back against the post, Mark lights his cigarette and begins to exhale smoke from his nostrils in two symmetrical streams.

♦ ♦ ♦

Picking up half the fruit, Eduardo offers it to Kirsten.

The blade of the machete has passed through the center, dividing it into two equal hemispheres, leaving bits of rust at the top and bottom of the cut. The edges are smooth, undistorted. Seen from one side, the fruit appears to be whole, a pale green globe extended continuously through all three hundred and sixty degrees, symmetrical in all directions. Set side by side, the halves are mirror images, mutually reflecting.

Balancing the peeled surface on the tips of his fingers, Eduardo gives one of the pieces to Kirsten. As he reaches towards her, his arm is repeated on the surface of the water, stretched into a pale white band that seems to float out towards the center, drifting away from the shore. The arm (distorted by the currents) moves sideways, as though the flesh (insubstantial, liquescent) were dissolving, flowing off the skeleton in a steady stream.

Kirsten accepts the fruit. Sitting back on her heels, she begins to suck the pulp, squeezing the juice into her open mouth. She works her way systematically around the rim, moving in towards the center, pushing against the sides. The sphere collapses into a crescent; the diameter is reduced, the circumference distorted, compressed slightly.

Look up, Kirsten smiles. Tossing the empty rind to one side, she says something in a low voice. Eduardo bends towards her. Her face (concealed by the shadows of the overhanging trees) is a blur, a screen of blue smoke, flat, empty, expressionless, suspended above the surface of the rock. As he moves, it seems to rise above his body, to condense into a mass of floating particles, an opaque emulsion drifting through a clear liquid.

(Eduardo bends closer. I watch his face drift slowly out of the shadows; I see it emerge section by section. Suddenly, as if some critical stage had been passed, all his features appear simultaneously. Every detail is perfectly distinct, clear, undistorted. Separating, the eyelashes form a ridge of hair that stands out sharply along the lower rim of the lids; the pupils contract slightly; there is an interreflection between surfaces, a faint flaring of the nostrils.)

(Closing my eyes, I repeat the motion, reducing it to a memory. Eduardo bends closer. I have the impression that I am looking at his face through an immersion lens. He drifts slowly out of the shadows, magnified, submerged, isolated.)

♦ ♦ ♦

Kirsten closes her eyes.

Upstream, above the bridge, the sun (sinking below the horizon) enters the shadows of the overhanging trees. Illuminated from this angle, the mist net is completely visible; each thread stands out distinctly revealing the entire grid.

The hummingbird has been removed. It is no longer possible (except by memory) to determine where the fruit lay on the forest floor. The net is empty. Dried by the descending sun, the threads move freely, swinging back and forth in the breeze. In the lower left-hand corner, a spider has built a web using the mesh for support. As the net moves out of the light (drifting back into the shadows, merging with the background vegetation) the web appears to be suspended in thin air, a double orb, expanded into three dimensions, connected to invisible supports.

The threads blow back into the light, billowing out over the water. The suture between the two orbs stands out distinctly—a dense, narrow arch. Woven in and out between the mesh of the net, the cables overlap, filtering the light through a semipermeable film of silk-like filaments. At irregular intervals along the net, other spiders have repeated this pattern. Seen from a distance, the webs give the impression of patches of moisture rising up from the forest floor, fog blowing along the edge of the river.

The pattern is repeated. As it blows back into the light, the entire net looks like an immense strainer, a screen that has been dipped into soapy water. The orbs, caught in the mesh, appear to be incomplete bubbles stretched between the threads, iridescent hemispheres poised on the point of breaking.

◆ ◆ ◆

Eduardo moves on the balls of his feet. He seems to slide effortlessly over a frictionless surface, to pass through a perfect vacuum. Eduardo leans forward. His head and shoulders are wet. Drops of water run down his back and chest in narrow, discontinuous bands, diverted by tufts of fine, blond hair.

The boy walks away from the pool. His body seems to respond to unconscious impulses, to be propelled by an interior force, by a reflex as spontaneous and irrepressible as the dilation of the pupils. As if following a pre-established pattern, he turns, deflected to one side like a particle passing through a magnetic field.

Lifting his head, Eduardo shakes the wet hair out of his eyes. The movement is prolonged, extended, as if filmed with a slow motion camera. There is time to observe every change in his posture, to examine the movements of his neck from multiple perspectives.

(Dulce-Maria opens the bag, breaking the bark strips. Bending down, she releases the snake. With a faint scraping sound it plunges through the Datura bush and begins to crawl towards the water. Shifting her weight onto her heels, the girl moves backwards. Halfway up the hill, she straightens up and turns around. The pool is no longer visible; the river is hidden behind a dense band of brush.)

As Eduardo walks towards the rock, his shadow appears to move a little behind him, stretching out in a long, continuous band from the edge of the forest to the rim of the pool. At its upper end (just before it joins the body) it is absorbed and partly assimilated by a lattice of moving leaves, by a complicated negative projection of twigs, vines, and limbs. These darker shadows distort the form, extending out from the forest like a border of raveled lace.

Stopping at the Datura bush, Eduardo suddenly leans down and pushes aside the bell-shaped flowers.

♦ ♦ ♦

The boat comes about in a long, slow semicircle. Despite the waves, there is almost no wind. Before the turn can be completed, it is hit sideways, flipped up in the air like a stick of balsa wood. Completely separated from the water, the hull rotates around an invisible axis, turning slowly counterclockwise. Then it is caught again, spun half way around, and flipped end over end. Kirsten is torn away from the mast and thrown out over the prow. She falls clumsily, her arms flung out to either side, bent at the elbows like a pair of broken wings.

As she hits the water, Kirsten dives, forcing her way to the bottom. Looking up, she watches the boat materialize above her, a blurred white oval that expands until it covers the entire surface. Individual details grow more distinct. The hold appears, a black cube filled with large, flat bubbles. Kirsten has the illusion that she is looking through a wall of green glass, through a sheet of colored resin that stretches above her in a dense, clear block.

Automatically, she begins to swim to one side, moving slowly with a certain indifference. Her motions seem mechanical, ritualized, a chain of instinctive patterns directed towards no conscious goal. Breaking the surface a few feet to the left of the boat, Kirsten reaches out with both hands and grabs a smooth, round object. Holding onto the boom, she pulls her shoulders out of the water.

◆ ◆ ◆

Eduardo leans down and pushes aside the Datura flowers.

(Closing my eyes, I repeat the motion, reproducing it methodically. The memory emerges as a perfect reflection, an exact replication.)

The boy bends over. Half his face is hidden, turned into the shadows. His forehead (smooth, convex) is partially concealed, covered by a damp, heavy cap of hair that conform to the contours of his skull. Only parts of things are visible—a single earlobe, one side of his nose, the outer corner of his mouth.

Eduardo opens his lips, touching the upper rim with the tip of his tongue. Lowering his head (reaching out over the flowers), he extends his neck in a straight line.

Seen from the side, the face appears to break into small fragments, to separate and dissolve. As he moves closer to the bush, his features blend together. Reduced to a triangle, the profile appears bland, continuous, uniform.

Eduardo stops. His body is bent like a strip of stiff plastic, taut, rigid. Hovering over the flowers, he looks like a large insect, an immense, fragile hymenopteron.

(I close my eyes. The moment is preserved, dilated, infinitely expanded.)

♦ ♦ ♦

Another wave breaks over the capsized boat. Holding onto the boom, Kirsten moves towards the shore, carried in on the crest. A line of cottages appears on the horizon, emerging out of the background vegetation.

Kirsten lifts her head and looks over her shoulder. From this position, she can see the hull, the mast, and the rudder suspended between two waves, drifting calmly in a patch of placid water like fragments of a broken shell. Nothing else is floating on the surface. Her brother is not visible.

Turning the boom, she tries to swim against the surf, to move back towards the boat. Her progress is infinitesimal. Caught by another large swell, she is pushed backwards. The cottages grow larger, more detailed; the beach becomes increasingly distinct, a sharp brown line running along the base of the hills.

Kicking out with both legs, Kirsten pushes against the force of the waves. Just behind her, she can hear the water breaking over a sand bar, the shallow sucking sound of the incoming tide. The noises blend into a single tone, sustained, amplified, increasing arithmetically.

Kirsten is washed closer. Lifting the upper portion of her body up off the boom, she looks back at the boat. Mast, rudder, hull. Nothing else is floating on the surface of the water.

◆ ◆ ◆

Eduardo bends over.

Suddenly, something appears at the edge of the bush. Lunging forward, blurred in the aura of its own motion, it seems to be a band of pure direction, a sharp, flat line without color or texture.

Merging for an instant with Eduardo, the line follows the curve of his body, bringing it to an abrupt stop, reversing its trajectory.

From a distance the boy appears to collide with an imaginary obstacle, to stumble backwards, pushed off his feet by an invisible wave. His motions are rapid, spasmodic, convulsive. On his right shoulder, just below the large muscles of his neck, I can see two symmetrical punctures.

(The snakes slides back into the bush, undulating, moving in a continuous curve. Blending into the flowers, assimilated by the forest, it disappears.)

The surface of the pool is smooth, clear, unbroken. On the opposite side of the water, several hummingbirds are hovering around the Heliconia.

125

As the air changes in temperature and pressure, the light inside the cabin appears to condense, to congeal into a solid cube.

Kirsten sits at the center, immobile, preserved like an insect in a block of amber. She sits on the edge of her cot, balancing an empty tin plate on her knees.

Color is replaced by sepia. The room continues to solidify around her, moving in from the edges. As the light decreases, the plate is reduced to a flat disk, a two-dimensional surface without depth or texture.

For a long time, Kirsten remains in the same position—defined by the space that surrounds her.

Suddenly, as if responding to a cue, noises begin. Moving up from the river, out from the edge of the forest, they penetrating the cabin, disturbing the internal equilibrium.

Approaching each other from opposite directions, sound and light overlap.

Kirsten gets up. Putting down her plate, she walks over to the table.

Without looking up, Mark selects another bird.

Books By Mary Mackey:

Novels:
The Widow's War, Berkley Books
The Notorious Mrs. Winston, Berkley Books
The Year The Horses Came (1st book of *The Earthsong Trilogy*), HarperSanFrancisco
The Horses At the Gate (2nd book of *The Earthsong Trilogy*), HarperSanFrancisco
The Fires of Spring (3rd book of *The Earthsong Trilogy*), Penguin
Season of Shadows, Bantam
The Kindness of Strangers, Simon & Schuster
A Grand Passion, Simon & Schuster
The Last Warrior Queen, Putman
McCarthy's List, Doubleday
Immersion, Shameless Hussy Press
The Stand In, Kensington (under pen name "Kate Clemens")
Sweet Revenge, Kensington (under pen name "Kate Clemens")

Poetry:
Sugar Zone, Marsh Hawk Press
Breaking The Fever, Marsh Hawk Press
The Dear Dance of Eros, Fjord Press
Skin Deep, Gallimaufry Press
One Night Stand, Effie's Press
Split Ends, Ariel Press

CPSIA information can be obtained at www.ICGtesting.com
Printed in the USA
BVOW071118250413

319125BV00001B/61/P